ISTANBUL

LUKE RICHARDSON

1

Uludağ, Turkey. Ten years ago.

AHMED SADIK PEERED out through the windscreen of his classic Alfa Romeo. The curving mountain road of Uludağ stretched out before him, tantalising him to go faster. One side of the road, the snow-covered slopes of the mountain rose towards the sky. On the other side, they fell steeply away.

The snow was bright and crisp. Sadik wondered whether it had fallen recently. Having lived three hours drive away in Istanbul for most of his life, Sadik only remembered visiting the mountain once or twice. He rolled down the window and cold air whipped into the car. The balmy streets of Istanbul seemed like another world compared to out here.

Sadik applied pressure to the accelerator and the Alfa's two-litre engine rose from a purr to a grumble. With the window open, the noise seemed to reverberate from the mountain itself. Sadik loved the sound of this old car. At the right speed, and on the right road, it somehow became a living thing. It was as though the car were in tune with the very road.

Sadik glanced through the side window; a few feet away a metal barrier flickered past. Beyond the barrier, the only break in the pearlescent snow was a collection of trees — just icy brushstrokes from here — shivering two hundred feet below. This high on the mountain slopes these roads could be icy too. Sadik applied the brake gently. The powerful machine obeyed, somewhat reluctantly.

He slowed further and cruised around a narrow bend, ice and gravel cracking beneath the thick tyres.

Sadik pulled into a single-track road. The Alfa's powered rear-wheels slipped for a few seconds on the seldom-used road. The car fishtailed left and then right. Sadik reduced pressure on the accelerator and let his speed drop. Then he accelerated up the incline, keeping the car within the worn tyre tracks. Experience had taught him that sometimes the best way to get somewhere was to slow right down. Speed often came with danger not far behind.

Sadik pulled up outside a wooden walled cabin and killed the engine. Thick snow blanketed the cabin's roof. A thread of smoke curled from the chimney and warm light radiated from the windows.

Sadik climbed out of the car and looked up at the sky. It was already getting dark, and here, far from the light pollution of the city, stars shimmered across the heavens.

"Mr Sadik." A voice came from the door of the cabin. "Thank you for making it all this way to see me."

Sadik looked at the cabin. He recognised the figure of Esin Kartan, the only woman on his executive team and the reason he had made the drive from the city. Esin leaned against the cabin's door frame and beckoned him in. As ever, she was impeccably dressed, her hair styled in her trademark precision bob. Warm light streamed out around her and patterned on freshly fallen snow.

"It's my pleasure." Sadik climbed the few stairs up to the cabin. Snow crunched beneath his handmade leather shoes. "It's nice to get out of the city and let her stretch her legs." He nodded at the Alfa Romeo behind him. The red paintwork shone especially bright against the backdrop of frost and snow.

"She is a beauty," Esin replied. "We don't get many sports cars up here. Once the temperature drops, you'll struggle with that on the mountain roads."

Sadik nodded. "I'll be back down before that." He glanced again at the sky. "Either way, I'll be fine. These European-made cars are tough as tanks."

"Of course. Come in, come in."

Sadik followed Esin inside the cabin. He scrutinised the younger woman, moving ahead with her normal calm and grace. During their phone call the previous day, she'd sounded uncharacteristically worried, almost frantic. Concerned, he had promised on the spot to make the long journey out to see her today. If one of his team had a problem, Sadik had a problem. He looked after his team, they looked after his company.

Sadik glanced around. The cabin was small, but cosy. Warmth radiated from wooden walls. A fire cracked and flickered in the grate. Two large sofas in deep red looked as though they could swallow a man whole.

"Can I get you a drink? I have wine, or perhaps a whiskey?" Esin strode towards a cabinet on the far side of the room.

"No thank you, Esin," Sadik replied calmly. "You know I don't drink. I haven't touched a drop in nearly twenty years."

"Yes, of course, my apologies." Esin turned and smiled. Sadik caught her eye. "A tea perhaps? I have just the thing."

Sadik replied with a single nod of the head and lowered himself into the sofa by the fire. The flames crackled and flared. Through the window behind him, the sun continued to sink. The rumbling of a boiling kettle floated through from the kitchen.

"Here we are. I can only ever find this beautiful tea in Antalya. Whenever I visit, I buy a bag or two."

Sadik accepted the steaming cup and placed it on the small wooden table beside him. He leaned forward and placed his hands on his knees.

Esin sunk gracefully into the opposite sofa.

"What's bothering you then?" Sadik asked, his eyes meeting hers. "It must be really important if it couldn't wait until we're both in the office next week. It sounded serious on the phone."

Esin cradled the cup in her hand and returned Sadik's gaze. She cleared her throat and then took a sip from the cup.

"It's about the company, sir. I wanted to talk with you about your plans for Sadik-Tech's future."

"Okay..."

"And I wanted to do it in such a way that was private. It's important that we maintain a united front, isn't it?"

"Yes, it is, of course. You know my door is always open to you. We can talk about anything."

"I'm worried about some of the ideas you were discussing in our last management meeting."

Sadik laughed, tilting his head back and opening his throat to the ceiling. "My retirement, you mean? You can just say it. You won't offend."

"Yes, I'm sorry." Esin smiled in return, then became

suddenly serious. "I'll be frank with you. I would like to buy your shares in the company before you retire. That'll give us a chance to transition properly and make sure the best interests of the company are served."

Sadik focused in on the woman. All humour disappeared from his expression. He contemplated his words and then spoke. "With the utmost respect for all you've done, I can't do that. This is a family company. One day, when they're old enough, I want my children, Ramiz and Xanthe, to be part of its growth."

Esin nodded, her eyes never leaving the older man. She said nothing for a moment, then nodded. "I understand."

"You know how much I've valued your help all these years, and when the time comes, Ramiz and Xanthe will, too." Sadik leant forward and touched the woman's elbow, his eyes shining at the mention of his children. "They will grow to appreciate you in the same way I do. Also, you already own a sizable share and will be rewarded for that as the company grows."

Esin nodded again.

"Now, let me try this tea. You can only find it in Antalya, you say? If it's that good, maybe we should send you there on business more often."

Esin smiled as Sadik sipped.

"Thank you for coming to see me, sir," Esin said, showing him to the door a few minutes later. "I'm glad we had this conversation and I am reassured by what you've said."

"That's good," Sadik said, stepping out into the night. An icy breeze passed across his body. He crossed back towards the car and shuddered, wrapping his jacket more tightly around him. He turned and looked up at Esin, standing at the door. "You know, Esin, this really is a beautiful place. Maybe when I'm retired, I'll get one myself."

"Thank you," Esin said. "Yes, maybe you should. We could be neighbours."

Sadik laughed, then opened the door, waved, and slid into the driver's seat.

The car grumbled and roared into life, headlights cutting a beam through the trees.

Esin heard the gearbox engage and the car crunch across the snow back towards the mountain road. She raised one hand in farewell and slid the other inside her trouser pocket. There she touched the empty glass vial, the contents of which had been drunk along with Mr Sadik's tea.

2

Istanbul. Present day.

SUNSET IN ISTANBUL. Both in Sultanahmet and across the glittering waters of the Bosphorus in Dogancilar, an unseen blanket of dusk was gradually being lowered over the city's daylight chaos.

In the markets and bazaars, the screeches of merchants muted in the growing shadows. Quiet negotiations in the cold buildings of Levent ended with shrugs and smiles.

The ghostly, high-pitched, sacred chant of the muezzin, which moments ago had boomed from the city's countless minarets, sunk back into the unquiet night. The faithful were already where they needed to be. Everyone else? Well, they didn't matter.

For this ancient meeting place, a fiercely defended confluence of the continents, night was coming. But night was not as pure as it once had been. Over the last century, desire and technology had diluted its power. Soon, darkness would spread across the sky, but not through the labyrinthine streets of the city. There, lights would continue blazing as the nocturnal circus bounced and bellowed its way through another turbulent night. It was a carnival that, to many, should have ended long ago. It was more trouble than the money that flowed in pursuit of such hedonism was worth.

In the district of Samatya, an Ejder Yalcin armoured combat vehicle, civilian issue, pulled from an underground parking lot. The giant vehicle's indicator light flashed briefly before the burly machine pulled out onto the road. A slim man on a motor bike raised his hand in protest. Then, upon seeing something through the thick glass windscreen, lowered his fist and pulled back behind the vehicle.

Not worth the protest.

Another identical vehicle followed, then another. The vehicles' sharp headlights cut through the late-autumn air. Reaching the end of the street, they turned on to the dual carriageway, which skirted the edge of the Bosphorus. The water was an inky black now, only the milky white scars of propellers indicated anyone was out there at all. On the Asian shore, lights shimmered through the cool evening air.

The three vehicles picked up speed, moving out into the fast lane to overtake a lumbering tanker. A taxi darted from their path, the driver squinting against the dazzling headlights.

Let them pass. No trouble here.

Three indicator lights clicked on together. Without breaking their formation, the vehicles moved onto a slip road. Sliding past the tourist sign for Sultanahmet — Istanbul's historic centre — the vehicles down shifted for the climb ahead.

Trams clattered and clanged past trees, withered by the chilly autumn winds. Groups of tourists mingled with the locals, seeking a restaurant or wandering toward the Golden

Horn. The nightclubs that occupied the steep streets of Galata prepared for the night ahead. In Istanbul, the night was young.

The vehicles geared down for the climb. Their mighty engines growled and thudded. Black smoke rose in clouds from their vertical exhaust pipes. Reaching the summit, they turned right towards the impressive towering forms of the Blue Mosque and the long-disputed jewel in Istanbul's crown — the Hagia Sophia.

The vehicles slowed further now.

A group of tourists watched the heavy vehicles pass before moving with disinterest to photograph something else. Tourists weren't a problem — they wouldn't think anything was unusual. Military on the streets was a common occurrence here.

Three powerful engines slipped into their lowest register, and the vehicles crunched to a stop. A heavy iron gate blocked their path. A thick chain secured the gates together and two security cameras peered down from long poles. Beyond the gate's vertical spikes, the imposing dome of the Hagia Sophia glowed against the sky.

The vehicles waited, unmoving, breathing hot gasps of expectant exhaust into the air.

A clang and rattle reverberated from the gate as an unseen hand yanked the chain from its fixings. Slowly, on ancient hinges, one of the gates swung open. A small man crossed through the sharp beams of light. He glanced up at the vehicles, his eyes shining in momentary illumination. He leaned into the other gate, toes curling in the soles of his battered shoes. Eventually, with an almighty shove, the hefty gate swung open. The rusted metal of the decrepit hinges screeched.

A guttural rumble issued from the leading vehicle. A

new plume of smoke rose from the exhaust. Thick tyres vibrated across the slabs. The vehicle pulled inside.

Orange floodlights washed the area in an eerie glow. The vehicles crawled in formation, following the rear wall of the building. Reaching a large door, they pulled to a stop. Three engines grumbled into silence.

The noise of the city swelled around them, the distant sound of idle chatter drifting on the breeze. Lively Turkish folk music played from somewhere nearby — a local musician maybe, plying his trade for the city's visitors.

The vehicles' lights remained on. All four doors of the front and rear vehicles swung open. Boots crashed onto ancient stones, worn smooth over centuries by the feet of the faithful.

Eight men exited the vehicles. They moved in practiced formation around the central vehicle. It wouldn't be the formation, however, that might interest a passing observer, but the sub-machine gun each man clutched to his chest.

Four of the men turned their backs to the vehicle and surveyed the surrounding area. Quick eyes darted between the bars of the fence. Sharp eyes examined each shadow and shift in the gloom. The other four moved towards the left passenger door of the central vehicle. The largest of the men stepped forward, extended his gloved hand, and lifted the handle. The locking mechanism clicked and then disengaged. The door swung open.

"Mr Fasslane," he said, locking eyes with the man inside. "The Hagia Sophia. We are here."

3

Uludağ, Turkey. Ten years ago.

AHMET SADIK SWUNG the Alfa Romeo in the direction of Bursa. The sky was black and clear now, the colour of the day having drained whilst he was inside.

He fanned his fingers in front of the car's air vent for a few moments. Hot air slipped across his skin, then turned cold. The car's heating system fought a losing battle against the sub-zero temperatures of the mountainside. Over six thousand feet above sea level, it was bound to get a little chilly from time to time.

That was the thing with classic cars, Sadik thought. They weren't as efficient as the new ones. Sadik tapped the walnut dashboard affectionately. He wouldn't change it for the world.

He powered around the corner and looked out across the valley. Trees quivered beneath a thick coating of silver frost. The moon hung ripe and low in the sky, as though ready for harvest. Somewhere in the distance, the lights of the town flickered.

There was something beautiful about the mountains, Sadik supposed. They were stark, bleak, unforgiving, almost... what was the word — he ran a hand through his greying beard — *sublime. Yes, sublime.*

Sadik pictured himself in a cabin like Esin's — cooking on the open fire, walking through the snow. There was something sort of... romantic about it.

Sadik shivered as a strafe of cold air somehow forced its way through the gap around the door. He changed his mind. *No, this was far too cold.*

When he retired, Sadik was going to move to the beach. Turkey had enough beautiful beaches to choose from. Maybe he would even change beaches every so often — just for the heck of it.

Yes, that would be much more agreeable.

Sadik leaned back into the seat and felt the imagined warmth of the beach tingle his fingers.

Perfect.

Another bend loomed ahead. A steel barrier flashed past the car's left side, beyond which the snowy mountainside tumbled into unlit valleys. On the right, a rock wall reared upwards. Snow and ice glistened from jutting outcrops. Fingers of frost hung down wherever they were able.

Sadik applied the brake slowly. His feet felt cold. Freezing. Almost as though they weren't there at all.

What's wrong with this heating system?

Sadik pressed at the brake again. Nothing happened. He glanced down at his legs. Something was off. Strange. Sadik took one hand from the wheel and rubbed it across his knees. There was no sensation.

Shock moved up his spine like a bolt of lightning. His

legs weren't just cold — they had no feeling at all. They were two blocks of ice themselves. Inhuman. Immovable.

He tried to examine them more closely. His neck moved an inch and then lolled forwards. He tried to straighten up, but couldn't. Panic clawed at his chest. He took a laboured breath and barely lifted his head.

A corner loomed ahead. The car increased in speed on the precipitous road. His eyes flicked. Right or left? Chasm or cliff?

He clenched the wheel with all his strength, his last vestige of control. His tendons bulged like tree roots. With all his remaining strength, emitting a desperate hiss of air, Sadik swung the wheel.

At first, the right side of the Alfa Romeo crunched into the mountainside. The headlights smashed, plunging the scene into darkness. Then the sounds of crunching, bucking metal filled the air. The steering column snapped, and the front wheels twisted at an unnatural angle. Sharp rock pummelled the right side of the car, bending it against the engine and splitting internal pipes and wires. Gas hissed and liquid sprayed. The forward motion not yet dispelled, the Alfa spun to the left, skittering body parts across the icy road. After a half turn, the car slammed sideways into the rock face. Glass smashed inwards, peppering the leather upholstery. The passenger door bent. A high-pitched screech filled the air as jagged rocks gouged holes in the metal.

The car rolled a few feet further backwards and then, in a hiss of deflating tyres, ground to a stop. Rocks fell from the mountain above, slamming like fists against the roof. Liquid pooled beneath the engine. Escaping gas hissed from somewhere.

The engine ticked gently. One indicator flashed an erratic pattern, filling the scene with a strange orange light.

All was quiet. Somewhere in the woodland, an animal called and scurried through the frosty undergrowth.

The sharp lights of another vehicle swept through the air. They lanced out across the valley and then swung in towards the wreck. A deep diesel grumble drifted on the breeze. The vehicle crept around the corner, Land Rover Defender, and picked its way slowly down the slope. Fixing the Alfa Romeo in its headlights, it slowed. The engine dropped into its lowest register. Gravel and ice snapped beneath the tyres. The Land Rover pulled to a stop ten yards behind the Alfa Romeo. Sharp ends of twisted metal glinted menacingly in the headlight's glare. The handbrake snapped on. The passenger door opened.

Esin Kartan strode towards the Alfa Romeo. She wore a large coat now, the fur lining turned up against her bare neck. Her precision bob swung as she reached the driver's door and peered in. Cocooned in gnarled and warped metal, Sadik stared back at her.

For a moment, it surprised her that his eyes were wide open. Then she remembered that the drug she had given him would just have rendered him immobile. Of course his eyes would still be open. He would see and hear everything around him — just not be able to react.

Esin smiled down at the man who she had worked beneath for almost fifteen years. No more of that. Now it was her time to lead.

"Burak!" she shouted back at the Defender. The driver's door swung open and a heavy-set man clambered out. The man walked over to the Alfa Romeo, his face set in a grizzled frown. The scar on the left side of his face shone silver in the moonlight.

"Get this door open." Esin pointed at the Alfa Romeo's twisted door.

The man punched in the shattered glass with a gloved hand, grabbed the frame, and yanked the door open.

Esin crouched beside Sadik. "Such a shame it had to end this way," she snapped. "I gave you the opportunity to sell to me, but you couldn't do it, could you?" She signalled for Burak to fetch something from the Land Rover. "You had to give those spoilt brats of yours the chance. Where was my chance, hey? I work tirelessly for you for fifteen years, and you want to pass it all on to someone who's done nothing — just because they're part of your disgusting family."

Burak returned from the Defender and handed Esin a length of plastic tube.

"Don't worry. This will be quick. Also, don't worry about your children. They'll be fine, as long as they're not as stubborn as you."

Esin forced Sadik's mouth open with a gloved hand. A gurgling sound came from the old man's mouth. His eyes bulged in fear. Esin forced the plastic tube down into his throat. When the tube was in position, she stood up, holding the other end above the stricken man.

Esin clicked her fingers, and Burak passed her a plastic funnel. Esin attached the funnel to the end of the tube. Burak handed her a bottle of vodka.

"Driving on these roads is dangerous at the best of times," Esin said, pouring the contents of the bottle into the funnel. The liquid slid down the tube and into Sadik's stomach. A gurgling sound came from the man's throat.

"To drive on these roads after a drink would be deadly." Esin threw the half-emptied bottle into the car, pulled the tube violently from Sadik's mouth, and walked away from the vehicle.

Burak slammed the driver's door closed and then crossed to the Land Rover. He removed a cable from the front of the Defender and then hitched it to the back of the Alfa. He climbed into the Land Rover and dragged the Alfa Romeo up the road. Metal screeched against the asphalt, dragging snow and ice with it. Burak revved the engine, positioning the Alfa Romeo in front of a gap in the barrier. A hundred feet below, snow-covered trees shimmered in the moonlight.

Burak stopped the Defender, got out and unhooked the Alfa Romeo.

Esin watched the scene from the far side of the road, her face distorted into a grin.

Burak climbed back into the Land Rover, revved the engine, and rammed into the Alfa. Metal scraped and screeched against metal. Burak swung the wheel hard to the left, forcing the Alfa from the road.

For a moment, it looked as though the little car was reluctant to go, then it wailed and scratched across the tarmac. Burak pushed the Defender harder. Clouds of fumes streamed from the exhaust.

The Alfa Romeo reached the precipice. Esin stepped closer to watch.

The front wheels hung over the edge. Dust and chucks of ice and snow rolled and skipped down the slope. Hundreds of feet below, a slither of open water glinted in the soft moonlight.

The Land Rover's engine growled again.

The Alfa Romeo screamed forwards, the body now angling downwards. The chassis rocked a few times before coming to rest at an awkward angle.

Burak revved the engine once more, but Esin held up her hand to stop him. She signalled he should pull away.

Burak clicked the Defender into reverse and slid back across the road.

Esin stepped up to the Alfa Romeo. She placed both hands against the remnants of the rear bumper and shoved. At first, nothing happened. Then, with a crack and a scrape, the car shifted.

Esin stood back and watched, her arms folded, as the Alfa Romeo slid and spun out of sight.

4

Istanbul. Present day.

ON PAPER, he was an insurance broker, working from an office in small-town Texas. He had the sedan, the wardrobe full of badly fitting suits, most of which were shades of brown, the pension plan, and the long-suffering wife and family. Heck, their suburban house even had the white picket fence to go with it. The American Dream surely was alive and well — or so it seemed.

Why that life might find him lying on his belly, on the roof of an eight-storey building, staring down the optical sight of his Barrett MRAD MK 22 sniper rifle, would take some figuring out. In reality, that alias was as fake as the passport back in his rented apartment, the sales brochures he carried, and the meeting he had scheduled with one of Turkey's leading tech companies. In reality, it was all a lie. It was a lie built on a lie, the start and end of which he had almost forgotten.

He was an assassin. He turned up, someone died, and then he vanished. But that wasn't the important thing — the important thing was that he never appeared to be there at all. He was as invisible as the air itself.

He was a necessary evil. An evil that secured the continuation of the right way. He smiled to himself beneath his black balaclava and focused on regulating his breathing. A heavy breath could upset the precise balance of his rifle and, from this distance, every millimetre counted. A hair's breadth over 400 yards was the difference between success and failure, and he never failed.

He scanned the rifle across the square beneath him. He followed a man and woman holding hands. They gazed up at the glowing facade of the Blue Mosque. The woman snapped a few photos, and then they continued into the melee of the crowd. He swept the rifle back towards the Hagia Sophia and adjusted the focus on the Leupold mark 5HD optical sight. He traced the line of the famous dome and settled on a pair of doves resting on the uppermost curve. He adjusted the sight, zoomed in, and focused on the flutter of their wings. His smile broadened. The poor birds wouldn't even know what had hit them. An exterminating force from another galaxy.

"We've got a visual. Three vehicles. Approaching from the south." A tinny voice crackled in his earpiece. He imagined the men, two streets away, cramped in the back of some delivery truck. He didn't know the men, and they didn't know him. They told him where to be and whose unlucky day it was.

He tapped the microphone twice — the signal for *"understood"* — then swept the rifle down towards the yard where the vehicles were due to arrive. The angle wasn't great. A tall fence with iron bars partly obscured the shot. It was the only shot he had with the necessary escape routes, though. It was good enough. He had succeeded in more challenging conditions — much more challenging.

He made a fine adjustment to the rifle. The bullet would sail between the bars as if they weren't even there. He only needed a moment. Less than a moment. He was confident he could make it happen.

Music drifted from the restaurant below him. Twelve feet away, people enjoyed their dinner. He glanced down at them. They were blissfully unaware that the lethal pop they would soon hear, and no doubt put down to a champagne cork or a car misfiring several streets away, was 40g of deadly tungsten moving at over three thousand feet a second, just a few inches above their heads.

"They're entering the compound," came the controller's voice again.

Again, he tapped the microphone. He would only speak in an emergency. Voices were identifiable. People who shouldn't hear it, just might. You never knew. It always paid to be careful.

He unfocused and then refocused the scope. Silently, and without looking, he checked the mechanism of the gun. Everything was as it should be. His gloved finger moved inside the trigger guard. His left hand adjusted the sight and the image enlarged.

The kill zone grew lighter. Bright white lights cut through the night. The leading vehicle crawled into his sight. He couldn't hear the engine from this distance, but he knew the sound of an Ejder Yalcin armoured vehicle from memory. His time in the desert heat of Helmand had seared the morose rumble into his mind.

The vehicles slid to a stop.

He swept the sight across them and then settled on the middle one. That's where he would have kept the target.

The powerful lights of the vehicles continued to blaze.

He smiled. They were making it easy for him, illuminating the target. They might as well put a bullseye on his back.

Men stood from the vehicles and moved around in formation. He recognised the guns they clutched to their chests.

One man moved to the rear passenger door of the middle vehicle.

The assassin's finger closed over the trigger. He felt the resistance of the mechanism. He applied pressure. Slow movements were essential. Too much could tip the rifle off target.

Slowly, a man emerged from the central vehicle.

5

Brent Fasslane stood and pulled a deep breath of the rich Turkish air. He was used to it now. He always thought that it tasted thicker and somehow sweeter than his home in New York. He should stop thinking of New York as home. It was unlikely he would ever get back there.

He glanced at the sky. The sun had not long since set across the city's jumble of domes and minarets. He thought about the call to prayer he'd heard while they were preparing. Although Fasslane didn't understand the meaning, he somehow liked the sound. It was the day's swansong. The last light's rite of passage.

Somewhere unseen, a siren wailed and then waned. A strong breeze charged in from the direction of the Sea of Marmara, bringing on its saline air the gentle note of burning incense.

Fasslane peered out between the bars of the courtyard. A moped strained past. Its bleating engine peaked and then faded.

"Sir." The man beside him placed a gloved hand on his arm. Like everyone in the organisation, his English was impeccable, although accented. Fasslane's eyes moved across the scar, which ran across the man's left cheek. "We've got to get inside. They're waiting for you."

"Sure," Fasslane said, glancing at a rooftop restaurant across the square. The diners were just discernible through the bars of the fence. "It's a big night. We've waited long enough for this."

6

Brighton, England. Present day.

LEO KNEW they intended to kill him. He saw it in their faces, in the way they moved in the shadows. These people, these things, didn't care who you were. They had one thing in mind, and if you were in the way, you were as good as dead.

He raised the gun to his shoulder, the way they had shown him half an hour earlier beneath the brightly-lit fluorescents of the 'Deployment Zone.' He looked carefully down the barrel. The thing was heavy, cumbersome and foreign. He moved forward awkwardly, scanning left and then right.

A light in the next room flickered on, exposing bare walls. Dark patches stained the bricks. A 'Danger, Deadly Infection' sign hung on one screw. Two yellow oil drums lay on their sides. Smoke seeped through a broken ventilation pipe.

A shriek echoed through the building from somewhere behind him. Ice shot through his veins and his breath caught in his throat. Footsteps pounded against bare floors.

The cry came again, halfway between animal and human. Something behind him rattled and scurried. Leo's heart hammered against his rib cage.

Leo spun on his heels, failing to keep the gun level with his eyesight, as he'd been told. He saw the creature too late. The thing half ran, half lumbered towards him, bulging eyes glistening and sharp teeth gnashing. In the pulsing red light, Leo saw it had half of its face missing. The jawbone was visible through a missing patch of cheek.

Lights strobed and flickered. A high-pitched, animalistic cry filled the air.

Leo fumbled with the gun, aiming it at the creature. He squeezed off a shot. The gun popped and recoiled. The shot sailed wildly above the creature's head.

The creature growled hungrily. The thing was nearing now. Light glowed from sharp teeth.

Leo's breath caught in his throat. He aimed square at the chest of the monster and pulled the trigger again. The creature howled in pain and reeled back, clutching its chest. Leo shuddered. The creature sunk to its knees, pain burning in its eyes.

A monstrous noise filled the air. But this noise came from behind him. Leo stepped back and spun again. Less than six feet away was another creature, similar to the first, except this one had an exposed bone where the left arm should be.

The creature lunged forward, a painful cry issuing from its lips. Leo fumbled with the gun. Two rounds pinged wildly around the room.

The creature cried again, lunged forward and then bright white light filled the room.

"Game over. Well done, mate. Return to the Deployment

Zone." A disembodied voice spoke through hidden loudspeakers.

"Who comes up with this stuff?" Leo asked twenty minutes later as he and Allissa stepped out into the afternoon air. Leo glanced back at 'Living Dead' stencilled above the door of the old industrial building.

"I don't know, but it was great, wasn't it!" Allissa said, glancing down at the sheet of paper detailing both hers and Leo's performance. "You know, you did better than I thought you would. You actually got the first two."

"Thanks guys," shouted two men, smoking cigarettes by the door. Leo glanced at them. One had a fake side of his face, showing a protruding jawbone. The other had a prosthetic arm with an exposed bone. The special effects looked much less real in the daylight.

Leo smiled and raised a hand, wondering if that would be the weirdest job ever. It was certainly up there, he concluded.

7

Istanbul. Present day

HE HAD A JOB TO DO, and he intended to get it done and get out of Istanbul as soon as possible. Tension forced his mouth into a grimace. His finger closed around the trigger. The mechanism clicked. He pictured the internal working of the machine.

Slowly, a man stood from the central vehicle. He was easily identifiable in the vehicle's bright lights. The close-cropped, oily-black hair and the thick neck. He even wore the angry scowl he had in the photo.

Target identified.

The assassin drew a slow breath and waited. He'd been told to wait for the instruction to fire. The line remained silent. He made a minor adjustment to the rifle, aligning the crosshairs with the target's forehead. He would have mere moments to make this shot.

The target turned, blinked, and looked out across the square.

The assassin let his breath escape slowly. He might not get another shot like this.

"Target locked. Permission to shoot," he whispered into the microphone. If he took the shot now, he would be back in his apartment before the body had even cooled.

Silence.

The assassin pursed his lips and exhaled. Moments ticked by.

The target turned to face the nearest guard.

"Permission denied," growled the controller. "We go after the event."

8

Ankara, Turkey. Two weeks earlier.

"Ms Kartan, the Minister will see you now."

Esin Kartan turned and looked at the woman behind the large wooden reception desk. The monolithic piece of furniture seemed to smother the tiny woman.

Esin rose to her feet and smoothed down her perfectly sized trouser suit. She'd had it made two weeks ago by her usual tailor in Venice.

Esin thanked the receptionist. For a moment, she wondered what it would feel like to be that meek.

Esin strode towards the Minister's inner office and turned her thoughts to the matter at hand. If she secured this deal, it would be the biggest in Sadik-Tech's history and would make them one of the country's biggest corporations. If she failed, well that didn't even bear thinking about.

Sadik-Tech had developed a system which, if rolled out nationwide, would see every woman, man and child registered on their database. The system would help log criminal behaviour, allow certain people to access public services, and stop those who weren't entitled to from operating in the country. It would also allow Sadik-Tech access to information on every one of Turkey's 85 million residents. In the modern era, Esin knew, information was money.

All she needed now was a nod from the powers that be.

"Thank you for coming to see me, Ms Kartan," the Minister said, glancing up as Esin strode through the door. He didn't stand, but indicated that Esin should take one of the red leather seats opposite him. "I trust your journey from Istanbul wasn't too laborious."

"Not at all," Esin said, closing the door and glancing around the office. "It was my pleasure." Secretly, she cursed the two-hundred-mile journey from Istanbul to Ankara. It made no sense to her that the government of their country wasn't in the far larger, much more interesting city of Istanbul.

The Turkish flag, its white crescent lost in the folds of the red blood fabric, fluttered in the draft from the door. To Esin, all at once, the thing appeared impotent and meaningless, mounted on a wooden pole behind the stout Minister. A useless piece of cloth gathering dust in an office — is that what a sense of country was now? She thought of all the times that flag had been contested, defended, killed over, and died for — just to become the backdrop for an overpaid civil servant.

The Minister cleared his throat, interlaced his fingers, and locked eyes with Esin. Beneath the frameless glasses, shadows bracketed his eyes.

Esin tilted her head to one side and smiled.

"Thank you for coming to see me," the Minster repeated. He tapped nervously at a document on the desk. "I have discussed your proposal with the President and our security advisory board. It's a very well thought out system, which we can see you have tested thoroughly."

Esin nodded. The proposal represented over a year of work, and several million lire.

"However, the government feels that we are not in a position to move forward with such a proposal at this time," the Minister continued softly. The man's gaze retreated to the safety of the papers on his desk. "We do not feel such measures are necessary at the moment."

A cloud moved across Esin's face. Fury burned in her gaze. A hammer struck her heart. Her eyes narrowed on the little man.

"With respect, sir, we are becoming one of the most poorly treated countries on the world stage. This sort of system, as the proposal sets out, would have us controlling our borders, increasing taxation revenue, and leading the way with the fight on crime."

"As I say," — the Minister finally met Esin's gaze — "I'm sorry it's not the news you wanted to hear, but we do not feel such measures are necessary at the moment."

"That, Minister, is a decision you will live to regret." Esin Kartan scowled, rose to her feet and abruptly swished from the minister's office.

9

Brighton. Present day.

"Hold on a second," Leo said, realising what Allissa had said as they crossed the road and ambled towards the seafront. "You didn't think I would shoot anything at all, did you?"

"I didn't say that. I just didn't think it played to your finely-tuned skill set."

Leo laughed out loud. "I'm pretty versatile, you know. Brains and brawn!"

It was Allissa's turn to laugh. They turned onto the seafront and crossed to the promenade. Summer had waned some time ago, taking with it the restless heat that had unsettled the whole of Europe for many weeks. Autumn was in full swing.

Leo noticed a man walking on the beach, a long coat drawn tight around him, a dog sniffing at his heels.

"It was good fun, though," Leo said, smiling.

Allissa didn't reply but slotted her arm through his.

The promenade before them was quiet. Brighton had

reverted to its normal, loveable self after the chaos of the summer. The city changed completely in the pleasant weather, Leo thought. In balmy summer heat, it became a caricature of a Victorian watercolour or a scene from a Graham Greene novel. Music streamed from open fronted bars and restaurants. Loud conversation and fits of laugher erupted from large groups of people. Antique merry go rounds competed with the clamour of street musicians. It was chaos, but it was friendly.

The colourful deckchairs, kiosks and beach towels that littered the beach were now packed away. The sky had faded into a sombre grey, and the sea merged from a royal blue to a strange shade of steel. Now, Leo thought, watching the breakers crashing and then dragging at the stones, it was the colour of freshly mixed concrete.

They wandered past the column of the i360 and Leo glanced out at the skeletal steel of the West Pier.

Like a peacock shedding its feathers, with the fading sun, the city became dour, serious, and once again, the place he enjoyed. Brighton was one of the few constants in his life. Whatever happened at the two-bedroom flat he and Allissa now shared, the city moved around them with reassuring regularity.

Leo and Allissa strolled in silence for a few minutes, both enjoying the sound of the sea and the sting of the air against their faces. Then, they crossed the road and headed towards their flat, two streets back from the promenade.

The Victorian building which contained their flat came into view. At some point during the twentieth century, the building had become three separate residences, and theirs was at the top. The place was small, but from the ancient sash windows, they could see the lazy glimmer of the sea.

Allissa had grown to like it during her time there.

A white van rumbled past them and squealed to a stop outside the building. The vehicle clicked into reverse and pulled into a vacant parking space, two wheels mounting the kerb.

Allissa pointed at the van, smiling. "Hey, he's in your space!"

"I know. Maybe he didn't see the reserved sign." After a spate of parking tickets totalling more than the value of the Leo's car, he'd finally sold it.

A man leapt out of the van, ran around to the back, and swung open the rear doors. He fumbled around for a few seconds, then emerged with a 'For Sale' sign.

Leo and Allissa crossed the road.

The man approached the front of Leo and Allissa's building, and zip tied the sign to a gatepost.

Leo and Allissa neared and the writing on the sign became clear — for sale, top-floor flat, followed by the name of the estate agent.

10

Istanbul. Present day.

HE WINCED as hot coffee splashed over his wrists from the three disposable cups he was attempting to hold.

A tram clattered and clanged, the wheels screeching against the rails as it turned the corner in the direction of Kabatas. He glanced up at the monolithic shape of the Hagia Sophia, punctuated by its four minarets.

Crossing the road, he muttered to himself as hot liquid sloshed over his fingers. He reached a side street and turned into the shadows. The flocks of tourists making their way to Sultanahmet didn't reach this far, nor did the garish lights of the city's nocturnal amusements.

He passed a launderette, closed for the night. The metal shutter was drawn down tight against the evening, blanketed with graffiti scrawls.

He squinted down the unlit street and saw a truck parked half up on the pavement. To the casual observer, the truck looked abandoned. That was the point.

An eddy of detritus skipped across the street. A cat

howled from somewhere nearby — an aggressive, hateful noise.

The man reached the truck and placed one coffee on the step to free a hand. He pulled open the door. Contrary to the truck's exterior, the door opened smoothly on well-oiled hinges.

A pearlescent blue glow streamed out. He snagged up the coffee, muttering as it burned his fingers again, and stepped inside.

"About time," grunted a male voice from the far end of the vehicle. "What took you so long?"

"Sorry, it took a while to find a place." He placed the coffee in front of his colleague and returned to his position by the door.

"Got sugar?"

He dug through his pockets and teased out the three sashays.

"Permission denied. Do not shoot," his colleague barked into a microphone. "We go after the event."

The man tore the tops from the three sashays all at once and dumped them into his coffee. "What is it with these guys, so trigger-happy? They just want to turn up, make holes in stuff and then go home. I've told him three times that we don't take him down until afterwards. I mean, it beggars belief that we're even in this shit hole at all." The man examined something on the screen in front of him and then took a sip of his coffee. "What is this rubbish?" he wailed, almost spitting the liquid out again.

"It's coffee," the younger man said, "just like you asked for."

"It's so bitter. These people really don't have a clue, do they?" He grimaced and took another swig from the cup. His jowls wobbled with distaste.

"Who is this guy, anyway?" the younger man asked, turning to his computer monitor. A stocky middle-aged man walked through a doorway and out of sight. Four armed military men followed him inside and the door swung shut.

"Above your paygrade son." The older guy looked around the inside of the truck. "But I'll tell ya, as you've hauled ass across the globe, you should at least know what we're dealing with." The man's thick fingers flashed across a keyboard and an image appeared on the screen.

The younger man scooted across to get a closer look.

The image was of the man they'd just watched disappear. It looked as if he were leading a protest. Surrounded by people holding banners and placards, he shouted into a megaphone. Tendons bulged from his thick neck and his skin pulsed red.

"This royal pain in the ass goes by the name of Brent Fasslane," the older man said, poking the screen with a fat finger. "He's been holed up here in Istanbul for nearly two years. He fled bail, charged with multiple counts of assault. Obviously, he claims the system is trying to stitch him up. I know what you're thinking —"

"Extradition."

"It's not that simple. We have someone the Turks want back. Some Imam who now lives in Florida. For reasons I can't even fathom, we won't hand him over. Anyway, in the last few months, this guy's been pissing off Uncle Sam a bit too much, so they've called us in. Total deniability and all that. But we've got a job to do, and here we are." The older man shrugged and chugged down the first cup of coffee.

"He must have really pissed off the wrong people." The younger man nodded sagely.

11

Brent Fasslane walked into the belly of the Hagia Sophia, and like everyone else — no matter how important you were — looked up in awe at the vast, distant, curving ceiling. Now, with the sun long sunk beyond the Marmara Sea, the windows were dark. Well positioned spotlights illuminated the room's great architectural and decorative features. The place had, Fasslane reminded himself, been the largest enclosed space on the planet for almost a thousand years. It had been a church, then a mosque, then a museum, and soon was to become a mosque again. Whatever those terms meant, and the religions that they represented, they didn't matter one bit to Brent Fasslane. What he had to say in his upcoming book would shatter millennia of religious scripts. Or so he believed.

Fasslane followed his security detail to the centre of the vast space's western facade. Now, in the dimness, Fasslane noticed that a temporary wall dissected the huge space. It ran from one column on the left to its opposite on the right and completely obscured the far side of the room. Six feet in height, the wall blocked his view of anyone on the other side, but allowed an undisrupted vista of the building's grand roof and walls.

The leader of Fasslane's security detail paused and muttered into his radio. A tinny voice came in reply.

Fasslane listened but couldn't understand a word. Then he noticed another noise rebounding from the ancient stone. A low babble rebounded from the hard walls, making it impossible to know what actual direction it was coming from. Fasslane stood still and listened. He focused on the hushed whispers. Now he could hear it properly, it sounded like hundreds of people whispering nearby.

"They're ready for you," the other man said, pointing towards the wall. His grey eyes bored into Fasslane's. "Remember, fifteen minutes maximum. We do this, and we get out of here. We're already risking too much."

Fasslane nodded, the excited beat of his pulse now rising above the sibilant murmurs.

The man pulled aside a wide curtain, revealing a brightly-lit platform beyond which hundreds of people waited expectantly. The man nodded for Fasslane to pass through, then lifted the radio to his lips. "Everyone at their stations, he's coming out. Remember, fifteen minutes."

"I got you," Fasslane said, stepping towards the stage.

12

Istanbul. Two weeks ago.

Esin Kartan's long fingers tapped an erratic pattern as the lift lumbered towards the seventh floor.

She was late for the meeting; she knew that, but didn't care. The other members of the board — all men and all totally full of themselves — would prefer it if she weren't there at all. That wasn't an option. As the Chief Executive Officer and one of Sadik-Tech's major shareholders, Esin wasn't going anywhere. Plus, she was the only one doing anything about their present financial shortfalls. All this bunch of stuffed suits did was moan about things not being as good as they were before, broker secret deals to sell their shares, and point fingers at each other.

The lift finally slowed, and then, after a series of minor adjustments, the doors strained open. The executive offices on the top floor of their building were quiet. Esin swept through the double doors of the conference suite.

Eight men, dressed in suits of grey or brown, turned to watched her. Eight pairs of eyes ran from her expensive high heels, clicking on the floor, up her trim body, and finally met her eyes. Esin didn't mind. She'd gotten used to the looks many years ago. She had her suits tailored in Venice twice a year with that very effect in mind. She took such looks as a testament to the fact she was doing something right. The 6am sessions in the gym with her personal trainer were gruelling after insufficient sleep.

"I trust you have good news for us, Ms Kartan," said the man at the head of the table.

Esin paced dramatically to the window and stared out at the city below. A boisterous afternoon had settled over the city.

"I'm afraid there has been a setback, Mr Ersoy," Esin said, turning and fixing on the man with one of her hard-eyed stares.

Ersoy straightened up in his seat, then pushed his glasses further up his nose.

Esin could see that he was already sweating.

A grumble of derision rose from the other men around the table.

Esin strode across the room and lowered herself into the only vacant chair at the table's far end. She slid a pen from her handbag and examined the documents on the table before her. The men imperceptibly shuffled in the opposite direction.

"You led us to believe," came another voice, "that you had this under control. In fact, in the revision of the minutes from the last meeting, which you have just missed, you said quite clearly this wouldn't be a problem."

"I may have many skills, Mr Osman." Esin pointed her pen at the little man. "But, alas, I cannot predict the future. I'm afraid the Minster is going to need a little more convincing that our product deserves a national rollout."

The men tutted. Several heads shook.

"Did you not make him understand the precarious position Turkey is in?" Ersoy demanded. "They have whipped us from both sides for too long!"

The men grumbled in agreement.

"The EU treat us like a poor cousin, our Asian neighbours give us nothing but trouble, and the Americans —"

"Yes, of course I did," Esin interrupted, the table shaking beneath her fist. "He knows the issues, but he is a weak man. He does not want to stand up and make the difference we do."

"What do you propose we do?" Osman said, leaning forward on the table, looking over his glasses at Esin.

Esin smiled wryly. For once, she didn't mind them leaning on her.

"Well gentlemen, of course I have a plan. We need to show that Minister how useful our system could be."

"Yes, but how?" Osman demanded, sitting back with his arms folded.

"We bring them a system that will help keep people in line, yes?" Esin looked from one man to the other. Each nodded.

"We need people to step out of line. We need some trouble, some panic, some chaos, and soon the government will be begging for our help."

The men around the table glanced nervously at each other. Ersoy was the first to speak.

"As ever, Ms Kartan, I am impressed by your nerve and ambition. What if this comes back on us?"

"It won't," Esin said, standing. "But just to be sure, you should take an extended holiday. That way, in the very unlikely event of any problems, you can deny all knowledge."

The men nodded again.

"How long will this take?" Osman asked.

Esin turned to face the men, glanced at her nails, then examined each man in turn. "Gentleman, it has already begun."

13

Istanbul. Present day.

WITH HIS PULSE vibrating his diaphragm and his hands clenched into fists, Fasslane took the stairs one at a time. If things tonight went as he and his associates planned, this would be a historical moment. He, and this night, would go down in history.

As he reached the top of the stairs, the rest of the Hagia Sophia revealed itself. An intake of breath echoed from the columns and domes. Fasslane looked out at his audience. Hundreds of people, seated in neat rows, stared back at him, unblinking. Then, Fasslane noticed people crowded in at the back too. Under the ornate arches of the building's main entrance, they bustled for space, elbowing each other out of the way. A camera at the back recorded his every move, as did two cameramen working the stage.

A moment in history, he repeated internally to himself.

A grin formed on his face.

Fasslane took a deep breath, straightened his jacket, and walked across the stage to the podium.

No one in the audience moved or spoke.

Fasslane placed his thick knuckles on the podium. He wasn't used to this. He was used to people shouting him down, belittling his theories, treating what he said like lies or parody. People rarely sat in stunned silence, waiting for him to speak.

Fasslane liked it. Tonight, he wouldn't disappoint.

Fasslane cleared his throat. Picked up by sensitive microphones on the lectern, the sound rebounded around the space.

He glanced up at the ornate decorations. Giant golden discs, covered with Arabic writing, sparkled in the low light. No one was looking at the building, though. Brent Fasslane was in the spotlight tonight.

"A new world order is coming," Fasslane begun, his voice strong and powerful. Honed on protest marches of the 80s and 90s, he knew how to speak to a crowd. "Most people don't want to see it, they are blind to it, they ignore it. But I speak to you today, as a man whose eyes are well and truly open. Whether you see it yet, whether you want it yet, a new world order is coming." Fasslane let his voice trail off.

During the moment's pause, he scanned the crowd. A team of black-clad security operatives melted into murky shadows at the foot of the giant walls.

"The governments of this world don't want you to see it. They don't want you to accept it. People like me, who talk about it, are discredited, or even disposed of." Fasslane listed several people who he believed had died under suspicious circumstances. "But change is inevitable. No man can hold back the tides. It is coming, and you will have to decide what to do about it." Fasslane held his fist up in the air.

"I stand here today as an American. A former American," he corrected himself. "When I burned my passport,"

— a thinly-veiled publicity stunt a few months ago — "I said enough to the rule of people who don't look out for my concerns. They tried to discredit me with bogus accusations of the worst kind. They tried to take away my freedom and belittle what I say. More importantly, though, they tried to pull the wool over your eyes. My ideas are too strong, too dangerous. I have spent my whole life collecting and cataloguing evidence which proves, without doubt, how greedy and self-obsessed our leaders have become. Like the fat pigs on an Orwellian farm, they feast on the spoils of famine, war and sickness, while the rest of us suffer." His face morphed into a solemn expression, and he stared at a point on the back wall.

"They see the everyman and woman — you and me — as objects from which to take their pound of flesh. To them you are nothing more than an asset to be used, and used, and used." Fasslane paused for a moment, reading the crowd. Hundreds of serious faces gazed back at him in enraptured silence. A thin smile crept onto Fasslane's lips — they were taking it exactly as he'd hoped. He was delivering the speech exactly as he'd been told. A professional. Fasslane took a deep breath and then continued.

"This is the same across the world, not just in my homeland. In Europe, in Australia, in every developed country in the world, you are just a number in a system, you are a digit on a spreadsheet. You are born, you pay your taxes, and you die. The worst thing, no one even sees the bars of the cage they're in. Anyone who questions, who searches for something more, is shunned, burned, discredited, even killed. But no more!" Fasslane's fists crashed into the podium. "It is only because countries like yours, and people like you, who have provided me with safety during this turbulent time, and are able to see through this, that I can even say this at all. If it weren't for you, I would be dead, discredited or imprisoned. Free speech is something we are supposed to value, but only when you're saying what *they* want. That is, until now." Fasslane extended a finger and shook it towards the audience. He checked his watch. He had less than five minutes left.

"When I escaped persecution in what is supposedly called the free world" — Fasslane's chubby fingers became quotation marks — "I brought with me all the proof I had collected. My life's work. These documents include records of bribes and profiteering of the worst kind. There are interviews with top politicians and business leaders who decided the truth must be told. Most of those brave men and women are no longer with us. Their deaths were not accidental or surprising. I share all this proof in my new book. Five-hundred pages of irrefutable evidence, verifying the constant and transparent corruption of our governments. I share specific details and specific cases where some of our most trusted men and women have betrayed us for personal gain. I give you evidence of the lives, money and reputations that have been ruined at the hands of this system. This is the system that had me tied to it by the nuts." Fasslane's voice rose to a shout. "Begging like a baby at the dry tits of capitalist America. Scrabbling around in the dust for... for..." Fasslane faltered. He sucked in a deep breath and calmed himself.

His head of security moved out from the shadows and fixed Fasslane with a slate-eyed stare.

Fasslane cleared his throat again and continued in a slow and even tone. "Many countries have already banned this book. More will follow. But here, in the free country of

Turkey, you'll be able to get it on every street corner. It is a testament to your leaders that they've allowed me to speak here today, on the eve of this building once again becoming a holy place. They understand what the world is becoming, and I thank them for their insight."

Fasslane looked straight down the lens of the camera at the back of the building. "You, watching this at home, before it is removed and banned from social media channels, or joining me here today, you are the last glimmer of hope for this world. We must rise against this oppression. We must stamp out this toxicity in our government like we would an illness — cut out the bad so the rest can flourish. I urge you, this week, find a way to get this book!" He grabbed the book from the lectern and held it aloft. "It's already been banned in several countries I know of, the large retailers will not stock it, but you are a creative, inventive, unstoppable people and you will find a way. Exposed between these pages," — he flicked open the book and swept through the pages — "are decades of secrets and lies, laid bare for you to read. Do not vote again until you have read this. Do not put your money in a bank again," he gasped. "Don't even buy a coffee again until you've read this."

The head of security looked from Fasslane to his watch and shook his head.

"Time is short, and I must go," Fasslane said, placing the book back on the lectern. "I am already in danger, and I don't want to risk the safety of the good men and women who have made this possible any more than necessary. But before I go, please hear this," — Fasslane extended his finger towards the camera — "you, learning the secrets in this book, is the last glimmer of promise for this world. It gives me hope that there is a place where freedom can be enjoyed. That, I am happy to risk my life for. Thank you. Together we can create this new world order!"

The sibilant echoes of Fasslane's final words bounced from the Hagia Sophia's antique arches. Fasslane nodded slowly, swept a hand through his hair, then turned and walked from the stage.

14

Istanbul. Present day.

MINUTES PASSED as he chewed angrily over the controller's instructions.

"Permission denied. We go after the event."

This was why he hated working with other people. They had no idea what it was like out here, lying on a scarcely concealed rooftop for hours on end. Then the perfect moment comes along, and they decide to wait.

What was the point of all his experience — years in the field, working private contracts, close protection work, building up his nameless support network across the world — all for some bureaucrat, sitting safely hundreds of feet away, maybe even thousand of miles away, to tell him the time wasn't quite right? How could you tell what time was right if you weren't even there? These idiots wouldn't know the right time if it put a bullet in them.

He cursed himself for accepting the job. He should have told them to stuff it and taken the trip to Switzerland as he'd planned. He'd be there now. A few weeks off the grid. Relaxing in a quiet alpine village.

He grumbled and squinted down the rifle's scope. A flurry of leaves moved through the yard behind the Hagia Sophia. The wind swept them up and over the dormant vehicles.

You noticed things like that when you did what he did. An unexpected wind could alter the course of a bullet from this distance. Clues for things like that were everywhere — a flag snapping at its tethers, or tall grass swishing from one side to the other.

Instinctively, he made a fine adjustment to the rifle. The mechanism ticked and then settled into its new position.

Nothing had happened since the men had disappeared inside. A few people had crossed the square — tourists probably — wandering back to their hotels or in pursuit of some nocturnal amusement.

A burst of laughter rose from the restaurant below. It didn't permeate his shield of focus.

He resisted the temptation to contact command. Radio silence was best.

His headset clicked and buzzed.

"Target is coming out. Shoot at the first opportunity," the controller said.

He tapped the microphone and set about rechecking, for the hundredth time, the gun's mechanism. He would be ready, just like he always was.

15

Brent Fasslane pushed through the curtain and into the rear of the Hagia Sophia.

The audience's stunned silence faded, and a rapturous applause began. Cheers, clapping and the clattering of chairs as people climbed to their feet boomed through the vast space.

Fasslane couldn't help but smile. The cameras would still be rolling, too. He had no doubt the stream would be taken down, but with an army of evangelists like those tonight, it would be reposted moments later.

Fasslane turned and gazed up at the building's magnificent domes and arcs. The gold Arabic script glowed pearlescent beneath spotlights. The whole place had an otherworldly appearance.

What a place to start a revolution, Fasslane thought.

His security men materialised from the shadows and surrounded him. The leader, his face set in a scowl, the long scar shining from his left cheek, led them back towards the building's rear exit.

The man was annoyed, Fasslane could tell. Fasslane had

overran by a couple of minutes. *Oh well.* Movements like this took time. He needed to give the people what they wanted. The applause continued booming.

The leader led them through an arch and into a passage at the back of the building. The applause dulled to a background murmur.

The leader paused and spoke hurriedly into his radio. He stared at Fasslane, unbridled dislike in his eyes.

"We move to the door now," he said, leading them away from the light. The four men surrounded Fasslane in formation and moved slowly, crablike, into the shadows. The leader barked an order and torches snapped on. Four fingers of light spread out around them.

The applause dwindled completely, and a tension settled over the group. Military issue boots cracked against the stone floors.

Fasslane looked out from the centre of the men. His adrenaline drained. In its place, a vague disquietude rose.

The leader held up a hand, and the men stopped. The leader's hand reconstituted itself with two fingers pointing forwards. The two men at the rear moved out to the sides of the space, sweeping their torches rhythmically from floor to ceiling and back again. Then the leader's hand pointed to the left. They moved in formation down a narrower passageway.

Following the men, Fasslane realised that he didn't know where they were going. He didn't think they had come in this way, although he hadn't been paying much attention.

The men reached a thick wooden door at the end of the passageway. Iron studs sparkled in the torchlight.

The leader turned to face Fasslane. "You know what you need to do." The man holstered his gun and raised a small video camera.

"Make it good," the man hissed. "We only have time for one take."

Then a new sound filled the space. It was distant at first, but it grew quickly. Something roared, grunted and groaned from behind the door.

16

He filled his lungs with the warm air of the evening. Incense drifted on the breeze. The fragrance of gentle spices and citrus cocktails rose from the restaurant.

He counted away the seconds, the way his training had programmed him all those years ago. In this job, everything could change in an instant. It was essential to remain constantly alert.

He panned the rifle smoothly from the right to the left. The three vehicles sat unmoving, their matt paintwork dull beneath the orange floodlights.

Forty five seconds ago, the voice had said the target was coming out. What was taking so long?

He focused harder on his counting, aware that the tension of the situation was reaching his heart and muscles. Nerves were the enemy of any soldier, particularly one whose quarry was half a mile away.

A new sound reached him on the breeze. The wheezing grumble of a powerful diesel engine.

He scanned the vehicles again. No fumes rose from their vertical exhausts and the lights remained off. It wasn't them.

He pulled momentarily away from the lens and saw a garbage truck lumber into the square. The vehicle moved slowly beneath the dappled shade of the overhanging trees. Orange lights strobed from the roof.

"Are you seeing this?" He hissed into the microphone. "Garbage truck. Is that supposed to be happening?"

He turned his attention back to activity in the yard. No movement.

Why was this taking so long?

"Yes, I see it," the controller growled in his headset. "No idea. Keep your eyes out."

He exhaled, barely keeping his anger in check. This operation was shambolic.

The garbage truck spluttered closer, thirty yards from intercepting his shot.

"I'm going to lose visual in thirty seconds," he hissed.

Static fizzed down the line.

He focused on the yard. The target should have emerged already. He adjusted the zoom and the door through which the men had disappeared over half an hour ago filled his vision. He focused in on the ancient wood, studded with iron. The thing looked centuries old, no doubt designed when enemies attacked with axes and arrows.

The garbage truck rumbled closer, its engine growling. Strobing orange lights filled the square.

He stayed fixed on the door, searching for any sign of movement.

A gust of wind swept through the yard. Leaves skipped in all directions.

He cursed the clear shot he'd let go earlier. The target would have been dead before he hit the ground. No collateral damage. That seemed like a dream now.

Then he saw movement. Slowly, the door swung open.

"They're coming out," he hissed into the microphone. His finger closed tighter around the trigger. He weighed up the rifle's mechanism.

Nebulous shapes swept through the night. There were three, maybe four people, all moving together like eels in a barrel.

"You have permission to fire," said the controller. "If you get a clear shot, do not hesitate."

He scowled and bit his lip. There was a word for people like the man on the other end of the line. He forced himself to concentrate.

The shapes moved towards the trucks, heads down, dancing through the shadows.

Then, as though teasing him, the bulky shape of the garbage truck staggered across his vision.

"Visual lost," he reported coldly.

"Did you take the shot?"

His blood rose in temperature another few degrees.

"No, there was no shot to take, and now the garbage truck is in the way."

Silence.

With the hiss of hydraulics and a final grunt, the garbage truck jarred to a stop. The engine pulsed through the evening air.

"You've got to be joking," he whispered, pulling back the zoom. The vehicle filled his vision. Rust spots covered the truck's once white paint. A layer of filth obscured the logo on the side.

A man in overalls climbed down from the cab, a half-smoked cigarette hanging from his lips. He shouted something up at the driver and then sauntered over to a bin. He pulled a sack of rubbish from the bin and flung it in the back of the truck. Finally, with a puff on the cigarette, he climbed back into the cab. The engine growled, then coughed, and the truck pulled away.

"About time," the assassin whispered. He refocused his lens on the yard. By some miracle, the vehicles were still there, their headlights now blazing.

"What do you see?" the controller interrupted.

A bright white light roared and rippled up into the clear night sky. The flash of light seared his retina against the powerful lens, blinding him momentarily.

He pulled away and blinked. Colours danced in his vision. A fireball rose into the sky, obscuring the city's skyline.

The sound followed. A howling, thumping noise that seemed to reverberate from the sky itself. Then metal crunched against stone. Glass shattered. Screams and shouts filled the air.

A wall of heat, dust and debris came a moment later. He closed his eyes to slits against it. A force pushed him sideways, knocking the rifle from its intricate mount. His gloved hands struggled for support. He slipped sideways across the roof.

He took a breath. He tasted burning plastic and fuel in the air. He pushed himself up to his elbows and looked out.

The noise of chaos rose around him. Shrieks and crashes boomed from the restaurant below him. Someone cried out.

He was focused again now. He assessed the scene.

Beside the Hagia Sophia, a fireball burned. Shadows danced across the rear wall of the colossal structure. At this distance, he couldn't make out exactly what had happened.

He snapped the sight from his rifle and clamped it against his eye. Realisation hit him like a punch to the gut. The central vehicle, the one the target had exited from, now blazed into the clear night sky.

17

Brighton. Present day.

MARCUS GREEN PULLED into a vacant parking space and looked up at the building. The Victorian house, like the hundreds that lined Brighton's streets, had been converted into flats. A 'For Sale' sign attached to the front gate vibrated in the wind.

A pair of seagulls pounded down from the roof of the building and tore into a food carton. Ripping it to shreds, and realising the carton was empty, they thumbed into the air again, shrieking mournfully.

You're not the only one to go without breakfast, Green thought, pulling a cup of coffee from the car's central console and taking a sip. It had gone cold. He glanced at the clock on the dashboard of his Mercedes A Class. 8am. The journey down from London had been arduous. The morning traffic was heavier than he'd expected. He had hoped to stop for breakfast, but couldn't risk missing his targets. 8am was a little later than he had wanted to get here, but he doubted these two would be up that early.

Green glanced down at a newspaper, folded open at an article on the passenger seat. Having spent most of his career tracking people down, he didn't expect today's quarry to be a problem.

Brighton detectives discredit Latvian future PM, the newspaper's headline read. Further down the page, a photogram showed a scruffy looking thirty-something man walking along a street with an attractive mixed-race woman.

Green didn't need the photo. He'd committed their images to memory.

He took another sip of the cold coffee and glanced around the street for a café to get a fresh one. Nothing was open. He finished the coffee, grimaced, and slid the cup back into the holder.

He picked up the newspaper and read about the detectives' most recent case in the Latvian capital of Riga. In true journalistic style, the article contained scant facts. There were a few rumours and a load of conjecture, fluffed out to one-thousand words. He would have done a much better job himself.

A bright yellow Mini slid to a stop outside the house. Green glanced up at it, squinting. The sky was clear and the sun bright, rending the luminous logo difficult to read. He snatched his sunglasses from the pocket of his coat.

"Active Lettings," he said out loud.

A tap on the window made him jump in his seat.

"Excuse me sir, you'll need to buy a ticket or move on," a traffic warden bellowed, leaning down and peering through the glass.

The door of the building swung open and the man — still with his scruffy hair — and the mixed-race woman stepped out onto the pavement. He glanced towards them, swore, and swung the car door open. The traffic warden leapt out of the way just in time, head shaking, reaching for his machine.

"Leo, Allissa!" He ran up the street, his voice lost in the rumble of a passing bus. "Wait, wait!"

The pair slid into the back of the Mini, the driver pulled out into the traffic.

He turned around and raced back to his car, just in time to see the parking warden peel off the sticker and slap it on the windscreen.

18

"I'VE GOT some great properties to show you today," said the letting agent, a blonde woman in her mid-thirties. She drove the car at surprising speed in the direction of Portslade. "It's always a busy time of year for us," she twittered on, raising her voice above the sound of some inert pop song streaming from the car's stereo.

"Thanks for arranging this for us," Allissa said. "At such short notice, too."

"That's no bother at all, don't you worry. We'll get you a place sorted pronto. It'll be smarter than that place you're in now. I can tell you that for nothing."

Leo ignored the twinge of insult that flashed through him. He liked their flat. He'd been there a long time and felt at home between the discoloured walls and threadbare carpet. The apartments they had viewed that morning were stark and bare by comparison.

The beeping of a car horn from behind them startled Leo. He turned and peered through the rear windscreen.

"Who is this madman?" the agent said, pointing at the car behind them.

A silver Mercedes drove mere inches from the Mini's bumper. The driver flashed the lights and sounded the horn.

"What is your problem?" the agent said, accelerating harder and overtaking a crawling bus.

Leo squinted, trying to make out the driver. Light patterned across the windscreen, obscuring his view.

Ahead, a truck pulled out of a loading bay. The agent accelerated again. Leo and Allissa sunk back into their seats. The Mini made it past the truck and shot through a set of traffic lights on orange.

"I'm so sorry about that," the agent said, reducing her speed and taking a deep breath. "I just really hate idiots who think they own the road. Who gave them the right to drive like that?"

"I'm impressed," Allissa said. "You drive better than he does, that's for sure."

The agent grinned at them in the mirror. "Blokes like that just really rile me up, you know?"

"Don't worry." Leo grinned. "Stuff like that happens to us all the time."

19

MARCUS GREEN SLAMMED on the brakes and the Mercedes squealed to a stop moments before colliding with a reversing truck. Dust pinged from the tyres.

The lorry driver, ignorant of the near miss, waved thanks from his window. The intermittent buzz of the lorry's reverse warning stopped, the gearbox clicked and the vehicle lumbered away. A cloud of diesel exhaust drifted over the windscreen of the Mercedes.

Marcus slapped the steering wheel and swore. Tracking these two down was supposed to be a simple job. Why were they so hard to find, anyway? They were supposed to be detectives for hire, not some kind of criminal asset.

He glanced down at his folder of research, thrown into the passenger footwell by the aggressive stop. He exhaled. This was a setback.

The car behind him beeped. He peered into the mirror. Now he was holding up the traffic.

"Okay, okay," Green said, snapping the Mercedes into gear and following the lorry towards the city centre. The yellow Mini was nowhere to be seen.

20

"This is the third property in this block that we've let this month." The agent leaned towards Allissa in mock camaraderie. "And I think this one's my favourite. You'll see why."

Leo and Allissa had spent the entire morning visiting various apartments around the city.

So far, though, none of the places had inspired them. Leo didn't hold out much hope for this one either.

"You're in for a real treat," the agent said, as the lift reached the sixth floor and the doors slid open.

Finding the for sale sign outside their flat two days ago had been a shock. When they'd climbed the stairs and found a letter explaining that the landlord had died and his estate was to be sold, it became real. They had one month to find somewhere else to live before prospective buyers would start traipsing through the place.

Allissa, not one to sit around, particularly while between cases, got straight to the task at hand.

The agent led them out of the lift and down a brightly lit corridor, twittering all the time about the various benefits of this building.

"It's an eco-efficient A-rated development. You've got basement parking," — Allissa glanced at Leo, grinning — "and access to the on-site gym and health suite." Leo glanced back at Allissa.

The agent unlocked the door at the end and turned to face Leo and Allissa.

"Honestly, I've saved the best 'til last. You're going to love it." She smiled and pushed the door open.

Allissa stepped inside, followed by Leo. A wall of glass overlooked the city.

"Now that's a view," Allissa said, stepping towards the window.

The city lay out before them — the Pavilion, the Palace Pier and the spidery remains of the West Pier, all backed by the glinting surface of the sea.

"I know, right?" the agent said. "Let me tell you, it's pretty rare to get a place like this."

Leo wandered around the apartment. It was modern, with faux wooden flooring, bright white walls and those tiny lights that are sunken into the ceiling. Leo tried to imagine his tatty furniture filling the place.

"It's really a blank canvas," the woman continued. "Once you've got your pictures on the walls, and your things around, you know?" She didn't pause for a reply. "It'll look like a proper home. It's got a modern kitchen, access to..."

Leo tuned out and moved towards the bedrooms. The stark decoration and lack of character continued in here. It was a nice place, on paper, but he just couldn't imagine himself and Allissa living here. He even felt scruffily dressed against the stark white walls.

"Thank you for your time this morning," Leo said when they were back at street level. "We've got a lot to think about now. We'll have a conversation and then get in touch with you in a day or so."

"Of course, of course." The agent shook her head. "Don't hang around, though. Things move quickly around here. Do you need a lift back?" The agent started towards the yellow Mini.

"No thanks," Leo and Allissa said in unison.

"We've got some stuff to do in town," Leo added.

21

Marcus Green pulled the car into a vacant parking space in a backstreet somewhere near the city centre. He'd avoided the city's vast multi-story car parks, not so much because of the cost — he would charge those to his employer — but because he knew from experience that once your car was in there, it could take hours to retrieve.

Green fed the meter a bunch of coins and waited for the ticket to appear. He impatiently tapped the screen several times. A curious seagull eyed him malevolently from the windowsill of a nearby building.

Once he'd displayed the ticket, he locked the car and headed towards the city centre. Having visited Brighton before, he strode for The Lanes. He would eat and then head back to Leo and Allissa's flat in an hour.

Green passed a vintage clothes shop on the left and one selling big-leaved tropical plants on the right, then found a café. He ordered a coffee and a sandwich, and settled at a table outside.

He put his phone on the table and let his eyes lose focus. It frustrated him that this had become so difficult. He should have been able to make contact from his north London office. He tapped impatiently at the table.

If the job wasn't so important, if this wasn't one of the biggest cases that had ever come across his desk, he probably wouldn't have bothered.

He watched a man with long dreadlocks saunter down the street towards him. A moped stuttered to a stop at the vintage clothes shop. The rider spoke with a woman in a tie-dye dress browsing the racks of clothes that spilled out onto the pavement.

Green hated to admit it, but he needed help, and fast.

The moped bleated once more as the rider pulled away. He watched it reach the end of the road and turn left.

That's when he saw them. Leo and Allissa, crossing the street in the direction of the city centre. They were maybe eighty feet away, but it was them. Definitely.

Green's hands made fists on the table, and he shot upright in his seat. Scrabbling his phone and wallet back into his pockets, he scrambled to his feet. The chair clattered to the pavement behind him. He darted down the lane, just as they disappeared out of sight.

"Get out of the way!" He bellowed, running down the street, his shoes slapping the pavement. He slowed at the last moment to avoid colliding with a woman carrying a tray of drinks.

He reached the end of the street and stopped. His heart beat furiously from the exertion. This street was narrower than the last. Shops spilled out onto the pavements on both sides, leaving only a few feet for pedestrians. He frantically scanned the crowd but couldn't see them. He examined each person carefully. Nothing.

22

"Let's cut down through The Lanes," Leo said, speaking for the first time in several minutes.

"Sure," Allissa agreed. "There's actually a shop I'd like to pop into."

Leo rolled his eyes. He knew the exact one. Allissa was building up quite a collection of crystals, weird talismans, and other mumbo jumbo from that particular shop.

"What did you think of those places?" Allissa said. Babbling voices drifted from somewhere nearby.

"Well, urrm." Leo exhaled. "They were nice, but they just didn't feel, you know, like home. They were all modern and stark. I'm sure we could make it work, but..."

"I know what you mean," Allissa said. "I'm going to miss our place."

"You like living in Brighton now? You don't want to spend your whole life running around the world anymore?"

They turned down one of the narrow streets. Boutique clothes shops, modern art galleries, cafes and pubs lined both sides. Brighton was alive, even on a weekday afternoon.

"I wouldn't say that." Alissa grinned. "As a UK base, it ticks a lot of boxes."

"A base? You call our home a base?" Leo rose to the bait.

Allissa laughed at his frustration. "You know what I mean. Don't do this whole emotionally wounded thing. In here," Allissa said, pulling them into a shop.

They emerged fifteen minutes later. Allissa stepped back into the midday sunlight, and Leo followed. He glanced at the small paper bag in her hand. He had no idea what the bag contained and wasn't going down the rabbit hole of asking. Any queries about that shop came with long and arduous explanations.

Pushing through throngs of people, they reached North Street and turned left towards the seafront. A police van rumbled past, spewing clouds of black smoke out onto the pavement. Several stone-faced police officers gazed out.

"What's that?" Leo asked. A noise rose above the grumble of the city. The sound of chanting voices carried on the breeze.

"I'm not sure," Allissa said, hearing it too. "But it's coming from this way."

The police van swung into a side road up ahead, sending a group of pedestrians running from its path.

Leo shuddered as apprehension moved up his spine. He glanced down at Allissa. Her eyes stayed focused on the street ahead. She quickened her pace.

"Hey, whatever is going on we're —"

"Not getting involved," Allissa interrupted. "Yeah, of course, but it's exciting to just have a look, right? Is that allowed?"

Leo and Allissa turned into the street and the noise increased further. Home to a couple of swanky restaurants and leading on to the gardens of the Royal Pavilion, Princes Place was usually quiet. Not today.

Twenty feet ahead, the police van struggled through groups of people, blue lights strobing.

At the end of the street, people filled the normally sedate pavilion gardens, banners, signs and flags held skyward.

The chanting rose again, reverberating from the surrounding buildings.

The police van stopped, finally giving up on its forward motion in the dense crowd, and a dozen officers climbed out.

Allissa stopped a young woman, striding purposefully towards the centre of the melee. "What's going on?"

"Haven't you heard? We want them to stop lying to us. We deserve to know the truth," the woman said, her voice raised above the crowd. "Governments, police, armies, the whole lot is based on lies. We deserve better." She pointed towards the crowd. "This is happening the world over. You won't see it on the news, though. Mainstream media will never spread something like this. They're in on it. This is not a protest, you hear me? This is an uprising." The woman disappeared into the baying crowd, threading herself towards the gardens.

A police siren shrieked from somewhere behind them. Another police van bullied its way into the street.

"Alright, we'll go," Allissa said, reading Leo's expression.

They turned and pushed their way out of the intensifying crowd.

Cutting their way down North Street towards the seafront, they passed countless people with signs and banners tucked under an arm or slung over a shoulder. It looked as though the protest — or uprising, as the young woman had called it — was only just getting started.

Leo and Allissa walked the twenty minute journey back to their flat in silence.

"I'm going to miss this place," Leo said, turning the corner and looking up at their flat. The bay windows on the third floor loomed darkly.

For a moment, Leo pictured the years he'd spent padding over the threadbare carpet and patching up the chipped wallpaper. Now, with the idea of living somewhere else in his thoughts, he could only picture the good times. He glanced at Allissa beside him.

"Yeah, me too," she agreed. "We'll find something we like, I'm sure."

"Leo, Allissa!" someone shouted.

Both froze in their tracks.

"You've been quite a challenge to find, I —"

It was a man's voice. Well-spoken and articulate. Familiarity chimed somewhere in Leo's thoughts.

"I've been looking all over the city. Don't you ever answer your emails?"

Leo and Allissa turned slowly. A man rushed across the road towards them. In his early forties, he had greying hair and wore a suit jacket with chinos. He was sweating and bedraggled.

Recognition dawned slowly for Leo. "I remember you," Leo said, pointing at the man. The memory formed more clarity. "We met you in Nepal."

"That's right," the man said, extending his hand. "Marcus Green. I'm so glad I've found you. I've got a bit of a situation and really need your help."

23

"My name is Brent Fasslane, and I'm going to die for the secrets I know." The voice boomed from Green's laptop. Leo and Allissa leaned in to get a better view of the video. The recording quality was indistinct and grainy. Figures, made emerald by the camera's over exposure, moved through the shadows. Feet shuffled and thudded against hard rock. A light snapped on. The small beam of a torch illuminated a man's face. Fasslane stood pale and ghostly in the tiny bright light. His eyes roamed, as though searching for an unseen pursuer.

Leo glanced up at Marcus Green. The man looked just as he remembered. They'd last seen Green giving evidence in court against Allissa's father. Blake Stockwell had been found guilty of a series of crimes, including attempting to have Allissa and Leo killed in Kathmandu. Without Green's systematic interrogative work, things would have ended up very differently indeed. Leo nodded with respect for the man.

"I've known that this was going to happen for a long time. My life has been in danger for many years. Too many people want to silence me. I know too much." Fasslane breathed heavily, his voice wavering.

"But please," he said, looking down the lens of the camera now. "It was only a matter of time for them to get to me, but this is bigger than me. This change, this movement, this revolution, this uprising... it cannot be stopped!" A shudder moved up Leo's spine at the echoed phrase from the woman at the protest. "It must not be stopped! Everything I know will come out, whether I'm there to see it or not. I implore you, if you're watching this, you must seek out the truth. You must find the truth... you must." Fasslane's voice trailed off. Shouting bellowed in the distance.

"They're coming now." Fasslane looked left and right, and stepped backwards. "They're coming." He looked directly into the camera lens. "I fear my fight is over, but you must continue this. You must seek out the truth and hold those who have caused so much pain accountable. The world is changing. I guarantee you that you can make it a good one."

The shouting came again, closer this time. Fasslane looked to the right of the camera. In the weak light of the torch, his expression paled further. His lips parted. A series of shouts rang out, and the camera fell to the floor. Feet pounded closer and then the camera went dead.

The screen of Green's laptop faded to black.

"That was broadcast live on Brent Fasslane's YouTube channel two weeks ago. No one has seen him since. At first, we thought it was just a publicity stunt around the production of his book," — Green pulled a thick hardback book from his briefcase and dropped it to the coffee table — "but there's been no sign of him since. You've probably seen this book on the news. Many have been lobbying to get in banned, others think it's the truth. They even debated the issue in parliament."

Leo picked up the book and flicked through the five-hundred pages.

"On the night he went missing, Fasslane was giving a speech at the Hagia Sophia in Istanbul —"

"The Hagia Sophia? I heard about that recently in the news," Allissa said.

"Yes, the government has just turned it back into a mosque. Fasslane's speech was one of the last non-religious events to be held there. As far as we understand, he's been staying in Turkey. The Americans have requested several times to have him extradited, but the Turkish Government has consistently refused. Anyway, this video must have come from someone on the inside."

Green tapped another key on the laptop. An image from a security camera filled the screen. Three military vehicles sat nose to tail.

"This is at the rear of the Hagia Sophia. Look at the time; Fasslane finished his speech just over five minutes before." Green pointed at the time at the top of the screen. A door swung open, and a group of men shuffled out. Shadows concealed their faces. Four of them held guns with the confidence of soldiers, and the fifth looked like a civilian. The military men fanned out in a practised motion. More military men moved into the shot.

The lack of sound exaggerated the efficiency of their movements.

"He's very well protected," Leo said.

"Yes, some kind of private security, we think. No idea who's paying for them. It's unlikely the Turkish army would help him in this way, although they're not confirming or denying anything, officially."

One of the soldiers led the civilian into the central vehicle. The other men swept the yard in a practised sequence before climbing into the trucks themselves. Strong headlights blazed from vehicles. Nothing happened for several seconds, and then the leading vehicle slid away slowly.

In silent slow motion, light flickered from the central vehicle and filled the screen.

Leo and Allissa gasped.

The camera struggled to adjust. For a few moments, nothing was discernible. Hot white light bleached the screen. The light faded, and the camera pulled into focus. Vicious flames leapt from the central vehicle and up into the night sky. Figures ran through the shadows in the distance.

"And that's the last we've seen of Brent Fasslane," Green said, stopping the video and folding his arms. "Or at least, that's what everyone thinks."

24

"It's very convenient. He's wanted by the Americans, then this happens the week before his book's released." Allissa picked up the book and leafed through.

"It's more than convenient," Green said. "Not only has this piece of largely unsubstantiated rubbish sold more copies than all of Dan Brown and JK Rowling's work, but people are lapping it up. In the US, here in England, all across Europe, since people got their hands on this book there's been a sharp increase in civil unrest, the popularity of fringe groups is soaring. People are taking their money from government backed investments, some are even refusing to pay their tax bills."

"What are you suggesting?" Leo said.

"Listen, I'm not saying the world is perfect. I know there are some corrupt politicians —" Green met Allissa's eye. "Sorry, I —"

"Don't worry," Allissa said. "My dad was a corrupt politician. Thanks to you, he isn't any more."

"I know the world's not perfect." Green cleared his throat. "But if this level of mistrust goes on, we're heading for something much worse. Large-scale protests, public services falling apart, the police won't be able to cope, people will have to protect their own property. It'll be ugly."

As though on cue, a police car squealed down the road outside. Leo thought of the protest they'd passed not an hour ago.

"You think there's no truth in any of the claims he's making in here?" Allissa said, flicking through the book.

"There is some truth in some of the claims, but this isn't the way justice is served. I've already got a team of people going through the book to see what we can substantiate. If it stands up, we will be handing all our research over to the authorities — that's how justice is done."

Allissa looked up at Green. The image of her father in court, pale, gaunt, yet remorseless, swam into her mind's eye. Green was right, justice needed to be served in the bright light of a court room, not the grim streets of one city or another.

"What can we do?" Allissa asked, placing the book on the coffee table and standing to meet Green's gaze full on.

Leo examined his hands in his lap.

"Hold on a second," Leo said. "You said, 'that's what everyone thinks.' You know something else, don't you?"

Green's face broke into a smile.

Allissa looked down at Leo. For a few moments, no one spoke. The gentle murmur of traffic noise drifted through the thin glass. A seagull shrieked overhead.

"We're not doing this unless you tell us everything you know," Allissa said. "We've had way too many people lying to us recently." Allissa and Leo exchanged glances, both thinking about their most recent case, just a few weeks ago in Riga.

"Of course," Green said, rubbing his hands together. "I'm

not going to keep anything from you. There are a group of radical journalists in Turkey, based out of Istanbul called, Gerçeğin Koruyucuları — the Guardians Truth. They're a mysterious bunch. No one knows who they are, but they make it their business to check claims made by government and big businesses in the media. I've got a contact there, no name, just an email address. Two days ago I got a link to this video. It hasn't gone public yet. I think they're waiting until they know more." Green tapped on the laptop and another video started to play. It was a shot of the same three military vehicles but filmed from above.

"It looks like drone footage," Allissa said.

"Yes, that's exactly what I thought," Green said, pointing at the middle vehicle on the screen. "Watch this very closely."

As in the previous video, the men appeared from the building and fanned out around the yard. Three of them crossed towards the central vehicle and got in.

"Watch now," Green muttered.

Leo and Allissa leaned in towards the screen. The vehicle's right-hand door swung closed behind the final man. Then, a couple of seconds later, the opposite door opened. Slowly, the men appeared again on the shadowed side of the vehicle. The camera zoomed in. Two more men emerged and crept to the rear of the vehicle. The leading man spoke into a radio and the vehicles' lights snapped on.

"They're dazzling the camera," Allissa whispered.

The men scurried behind the rear vehicle and out of the shot. The drone footage zoomed out again, but they had dissolved into the shadows of the building.

"That footage was a set up," Leo said as the vehicle on the screen exploded.

"Yep," Green said, stopping the video. "Fasslane wants us

to think he's been assassinated, because that reinforces the claims he makes in here." Green picked up the book and brandished it like a weapon. "Of course, my team are working to disprove the information in here, but that could take months. There are over five hundred pages."

"People are already rioting about this. We don't have months." Allissa looked from the book to Leo.

"This isn't a protest, this is an uprising," Leo whispered.

25

"Where do we even begin?" Allissa asked a few minutes later. Empty coffee cups had been refilled and laptops readied for the research process.

"We need to know everything we can about Fasslane," Leo said. "Where did he come from? What took him to Istanbul? All of that."

Green took a sip of his coffee and turned back from the window. "I can tell you all of this. I've been watching this guy for years. He was always going to be trouble." Green pulled a chair from beneath the dining table and sat facing Leo and Allissa. For the next ten minutes, Green ran through all he knew about Fasslane, from his beginnings as a reporter for a right-wing newspaper in New York, to his fleeing the US and finding safety in Turkey.

Leo was impressed by how succinctly the journalist could express large amounts of information. Allissa took notes.

"Have you any idea of where he could be now?" Leo asked when Green had finished.

"He's been in Istanbul a long time, there's no knowing

what contacts he's made in that period. I know where we need to start, though."

"Where?" Allissa asked, exchanging a momentary glance with Leo.

"The Guardians of Truth," Green said. "We need to get to Istanbul and make contact with them. Something tells me this video is just the start."

Leo and Allissa nodded.

"Okay." Leo looked hard at Green. Whilst he liked and respected the man, there was one rule he wasn't breaking again. "But Allissa and I work alone."

26

Istanbul. Present day.

"You're working late tonight boss,"

Esin Kartan looked up from the screen of her computer and towards the gruff voice at the door. Her office, on the top floor of the Sadik-Tech building in Samatya, had grown dark with the setting sun. Everyone else on the floor had gone home long ago.

Absorbed in what she was doing, Esin had hardly noticed.

She recognised the muscular figure of her security chief and fixer, Burak. The scar which ran down the left side of Burak's face, giving him something of a permanent frown, shone in some distant light.

"Yes, I suppose I am," Esin said warmly. Of all the people in the organisation, Burak was the only one she trusted. All the others, the slimy men on the board, were just in it for what they could get out of it.

Esin watched Burak cross the room, thick arms hanging by his sides. Esin smiled. Although Burak looked like a thug, he was loyal to the core and, as proven in the last few weeks, could be trusted to get the job done.

A siren screamed from the street below. It was quickly joined by another.

Esin watched Burak closely and wondered if he would actually die for her. For a fleeting second, she hoped she wouldn't have to find out.

"But, when you're enjoying the job this much, it doesn't really feel like work. Come and have a look at this." Esin pointed towards the screen in front of her.

Burak lumbered around the desk. Esin wasn't sure she had ever seen him wearing anything but the same dreary black clothes.

"People are rioting all over the world, see?" She flicked through several browsers. "London. Tokyo. Berlin. Cape Town. All sorts of places."

"All because of him?" Burak asked.

Esin nodded and a giggle escaped her lips. "They're taking his disappearance as a sign that what he says is true."

Burak's face twisted into a snarl. On the screen, police clashed with protesters in Sydney.

"People can be so predictable," Esin said, her smile broadening further. "Some blame the Americans, others blame the Turkish, but no one really knows. A few months, or maybe even weeks of this, and they'll be paying anyone to help clear up the mess."

27

A LATE AFTERNOON haze had settled over Istanbul as Leo and Allissa's taxi pulled into a Sultanahmet backstreet. The driver stopped the taxi and pointed out through the windscreen. Leo and Allissa didn't understand his words, but it was clear that they'd reached their destination.

Leo paid the driver, then they bundled out, grabbed their bags from the boot and wandered up the street in search of their apartment. Haphazard four storey buildings flanked the street on both sides. A hotel sat beside a small café, whose chairs and tables spilled out onto the pavement. Allissa paused to watch a pair of cats darting playfully across the street. Their fur was glossy and bright — like those kept as pets by many of her friends.

Allissa thought for a moment about what it would be like to have one themselves. She liked the idea, but knew that the complexity of not being able to leave them alone for more than a few hours would drive her mad.

The flight from London Gatwick had been uneventful. Leo had watched Europe sliding beneath, whilst Allissa snored sweetly. As usual, Leo was now exhausted, and Allissa was full of boundless energy.

"There it is," Allissa said, pointing at a door further up the street. Leo trudged up the incline behind her, then looked up at the building. The building was unremarkable from its neighbours — bars covered the windows on the ground floor, satellite dishes and air conditioners sprouted beside each of the windows above.

Allissa poked the intercom mounted on the right of the thick black door. A buzzer sounded from somewhere deep within the building. A voice rose a moment later, followed by the patter of footsteps. The lock clicked, and the door swung open to reveal a wide-hipped woman with short red hair and a mobile phone clamped to her ear.

"Hi," Allissa said, smiling. "We're staying —"

"No English," the woman barked, beckoning them it. Without a break in her one-sided conversation, the woman led them up the stairs. Allissa glanced at the woman's feet, clad in a dirty pair of flip-flops flapping against the tiles.

Since the tiny place Leo arranged for them in Hong Kong, Allissa had taken charge of arranging their accommodations. She was skilled at both finding good quality places, but without paying too much. Climbing the dingy staircase, though, Allissa doubted her choice. Maybe she should have gone for one of the large hotels nearby. She turned around and caught Leo's eye. He grinned in a way that said he doubted it too.

Dirty water streaked the floor, and the only light came from a naked bulb hanging on a wire.

On the third floor, still without a break in her monologue, the woman pointed at a door at the end of the hall.

Leo and Allissa stepped over a mop and bucket, and

shuffled towards the door. Allissa felt sorry for the person on the other end of the phone.

The door was unlocked. Leo pushed through the door and into the apartment that was to be their home for the next few days. Allissa dropped her bag to the bed. Leo put his bag down and looked around. The place was a simple one-room studio, with a double bed and a compact kitchenette. One door led through to the bathroom, and the other to a small terrace.

"Not bad," Leo said, glancing at Allissa. The voice of the red-haired woman faded with the sound of her descending flip flops.

"I thought you'd approve," Allissa said, pulling off her shoes. "It was a bargain."

Leo strode to the far end of the room and swung open a glass door.

"Balcony, nice!" he shouted back after stepping through. The terrace looked out across the disordered roofs of downtown Istanbul. Block concrete buildings jostled for space beside the slender minarets and domes of a nearby mosque. Rusting antennas bristled upwards amid webs of tangled wire. Multicoloured washing hung on several rooftops, flapping lethargically.

In one direction the sea of Marmara glinted, in the other the ancient slopes of Sultanahmet and the centre of ancient Istanbul crouched ready for exploration.

Allissa stepped out onto the terrace too, squinting in the sharp autumn sunlight.

"Cool place, isn't —"

Allissa stopped talking as the call to prayer boomed from the mosque at the end of the street. A ghostly voice fluctuated in pitch, the meaning of the words lost on Leo and Allissa. "I wonder what they're saying?" Allissa whispered.

Leo slipped his hand around Allissa's and turned to face the minarets of the mosque at the end of the street.

"Afternoon prayers," Leo said with a grin. "How many times a day do you think they'll do that?" he asked.

"Five," Allissa said, returning his smile. "At least."

28

Allissa peered up at the muscular outline of the Hagia Sophia. The building towered above them, its stocky dome and minarets silhouetted against the afternoon sky.

After dropping their bags at the apartment, Leo and Allissa had headed straight here, intending to check out the place where Brent Fasslane was last seen. Allissa didn't imagine the visit would reveal anything in the way of actual clues, but just getting a feeling of the place was important.

The snaking line shuffled towards the security checkpoint. Leo and Allissa took a step forward.

Allissa turned and studied the vast square behind them. The square was the centre of Istanbul's tourist district and a circus of activity in the early afternoon. Tourists milled around, clutching maps and cameras while circled by touts and hawkers. To the left side of the melee, the minarets of the Blue Mosque stretched upwards. To the right, the Obelisk of Theodosius dwarfed passing tourists, many unaware that it pre-dated the surrounding buildings by several thousand years. For a moment, as she often did when in historical sights, Allissa wondered what incredible stories the 60-foot spire of stone could tell. The thing had seen the rise and fall of empires more than once.

A tram clanged around a corner nearby, drawing Allissa's attention. She looked towards the sound. Allissa followed the tram as it dinged and rumbled down the incline towards the Golden Horn. Commuters gazed mindlessly through the glass.

Then, as the tram disappeared beyond a wall, Allissa caught the gaze of a man standing about fifty feet away. He wore blue jeans and a black jacket, and had dark hair and olive skin. He appeared to have no purpose in the tourist melee of the square. He held her gaze for a moment, before looking away and melting into the crowd.

Allissa watched him go, worry etching her brow. There was something about the look that had startled her. Allissa continued to stare into the place where the man had been. Maybe she was just seeing things? She shook her head, as though to clear the thought. Maybe he was just looking for someone he knew in the crowd.

"Come on," Leo said, pulling Allissa through the gates and into the security checkpoint.

A few minutes later, they stepped between thick wooden doors and into the cool interior of the Hagia Sophia. Colours danced across Allissa's vision. A wide stone corridor led deeper into the building. Allissa's eyes adjusted. She gazed up at the walls, painted with frescos of red and gold. She stopped to examine each painting in turn, imagining what story it told. The intricate detail, hinted at civilizations of the past.

They shuffled on through another set of doors and into a larger room. This one had a high arched ceiling. Light streamed in thick bars from small high windows. The air was cooler inside. Allissa's eyes widened with wonder and awe. She turned one way and then the other, not wanting to move on.

Leo dragged her on into the ancient building's main room. Allissa and Leo stepped forwards, their necks craning to take in the enormity of the place. The dome, glowing in gold and bronze, shimmered far above them. Great discs adorned with Arabic script hung around the walls.

"Wow! Crazy, isn't it?" Leo whispered in Allissa's ear.

Leo and Allissa walked across the giant room, their feet sinking into the carpet. Lights hung on long chains, illuminating the stone in a soft, golden glow.

Reaching the far end of the building, Leo dug out his phone. He scrolled through the recording of Brent Fasslane's speech. He looked from the screen to the surrounding building, trying to figure out the layout of the room.

"It looks like the stage was there." Leo pointed to an area in the centre.

Allissa leaned in and strained to see the video. "Go back to the start. Where did Fasslane enter and leave?"

Leo scrolled back through the video. "You can't see clearly because of that curtain, but I suspect it was there," he said, pointing to an arch in the back corner.

Allissa led them across the room. The arch led into a shadowy passageway. A velvet rope hung across it. Allissa peered into the darkness.

"That must lead out to the back of the building, where we saw Fasslane leave," Leo said.

Allissa nodded, then turned and glanced around the room behind them. She froze. Standing on the far side, gazing disinterestedly at a wall, was the man she'd seen outside. The same slight frame, black jacket, blue jeans.

"That man, over by that pillar," Allissa said, glancing

quickly across the room. "He was watching us outside, I'm sure of it. He caught my eye in the line."

Leo feigned a look around the interior to examine him. "Do you think he's following us?"

"Maybe. He's definitely interested in what we're doing."

The man's stance shifted. He strolled nonchalantly across the room and looked up at the opposite wall.

"Let's give him something to be interested in," Allissa said, unclipping the velvet rope and slipping inside the passageway.

"We can't do —" Leo stopped in mid-sentence. Allissa had already started running into the darkness.

29

"This way," Allissa whispered, pointing deeper into the passageway. Her voice sounded loud in the enclosed space.

Leo glanced over his shoulder. The Hagia Sophia's main room was forty feet behind them now. Tourists milled about, their necks craned as they examined the vast dome. Leo's pulse quickened as he thought about the armed guards they'd passed at the entrance. Every inch of this place must be covered by security cameras.

They ran on, their footsteps reverberating from bare stone walls and ceiling. The passage curved to the left. The shadows became thicker.

Twenty feet further, a single bulb hung from the ceiling. A thick wooden door stood in the island of light.

Certain it would be locked, forcing them to retreat back towards the armed men, Leo felt the rising sting of anxiety. It closed around his chest like a squeezing pair of hands.

Allissa reached the door first and drew back two rusting bolts. Leo joined her and together they tugged on the door. With a screech of decrepit hinges, the door swung open.

Daylight streamed in. Leo blinked.

Then he heard the deafening thud of boots on the stone floors behind them.

"Quickly," Leo panted, charging through. "Get this closed."

Leo and Allissa heaved the door shut. The thumping boots sunk to a dull knock.

"I can't believe you made us do that," Leo said breathlessly. He bent double and tried to pull a deep breath.

Allissa looked around at the courtyard.

"That guy had probably just come to see the place. For once you're the one who's seeing things."

"No, there was definitely something about him," Allissa said, glancing around. "Hey, this is where —" She pointed out into the courtyard, and then looked up at a security camera on the wall above them. Singed branches hung overhead.

Raised voices howled through the closed door behind them now.

"We need to get out of here," Leo hissed, straightening up. He rushed over to the gate, pulled back the lock and dragged it open.

A bus rumbled past. Leo got a lungful of exhaust fumes.

Leo and Allissa stepped through the gate and merged into a crowd of tourists a moment before a pair of armed security guards burst out into the courtyard.

"I can't believe you did that to us," Leo said. They'd wandered across the Golden Horn and were now sitting outside a bar three streets away from the Galata Tower.

"It was fine." Allissa lifted a bottle of cold Efes beer to her lips. Leo's sat on the table, still untouched.

"It might not have been. Those security guards were armed. They could have shot us." Leo's hands curled like claws.

"They weren't going to shoot us," Allissa said, fixing him with a stare. "If they caught up with us, we would have just said we were lost. People don't go around shooting tourists."

"This isn't a game." His hands balled into fists now. "This is serious stuff. People do get shot and I —" His breath caught in his throat.

Allissa watched him from the other side of the table. She didn't say anything. Silence swelled between the couple. Allissa scowled, frustration boiling inside her. She took another sip from the beer.

A delivery van rolled past and stopped outside the shop next door.

"At least we got to see the place where they rigged the explosion," Allissa said softly. She finished her beer and signalled the waiter for another.

"Yeah, we did," Leo said, catching her eye for the first time since they'd run. "Maybe I overreacted a bit there,"

Allissa reached out and touched his hands, which were now laying colourless and flat on the table.

"You're right," Allissa said, glancing up at the strip of sky which was turning crimson. "I shouldn't have done that. It was dangerous and reckless. It was that guy —"

"Do you think you'd recognise him again?" Leo asked. He finally lifted the beer and took a long sip.

"I think so," Allissa said. "It might be nothing, but —"

"Oh right, so now you say it might be nothing, after you've had us running through the restricted areas of an ancient monument." Leo grinned.

Allissa laughed cheerlessly as she looked at her empty beer bottle. "I don't know," she said, flicking the label with her thumb. "He just caught my eye. It was strange. It wasn't like a casual stare. He was definitely watching us. I had a feeling."

"We'll keep an eye out," Leo reassured. Whilst he didn't share Allissa's concern — she was a beautiful woman who men glanced at frequently — he knew that in their line of work, instincts were vital. You ignored them at your peril.

An electric car hummed past the café, pausing for a group of teenagers to cross the road. The fruit seller on the opposite side of the road lugged crates of grapefruits and pomegranates back inside. Many of the shops were already closed for the night, brightly coloured shutters locked across their front windows.

A cool breeze pushed up the narrow street, bringing with it the sweet smell of sizzling spice.

"We've lost him for now, anyway." Leo reached across the table and put his hand on Allissa's. The final ravages of the anxiety drained from his system. "Let's get some food, then we'll get a taxi back to the apartment."

30

"You've definitely got the key." Leo rummaged through his pockets with one hand, holding two bottles of beer with the other. Allissa climbed the stairs in front of him.

"I definitely don't," Allissa said as she reached the door.

"Hold these." Leo passed across the beers and ran his hands down over his trousers. Sure enough, the apartment key was in his back pocket, attached to a sizable chuck of wood.

Leo opened the door and switched on the ceiling fan. Allissa carried the beers out onto the balcony. Blue lights washed the ornate domes of the nearby mosque, and the Sea of Marmara glinted.

"Not bad at all, is it?" Leo said, stepping out onto the terrace. "It's not as bad as I first thought."

Allissa nodded. The beautiful Turkish food and several ice-cold beers had almost quelled her earlier frustrations.

"Let's get these beers open." Leo snagged up one of the bottles and attempted to twist off the top. It wouldn't move.

"You'll need an opener," Allissa said.

"No, I saw the barman earlier do it like this." Leo tried again and then winced as the top cut into his palm.

"Well, he was obviously stronger than you. Don't hurt yourself. I'll get an opener." Allissa stepped inside, grinning. She snapped on the kitchen light.

Her body froze in position. Ice ran through her veins. She tried to catch her breath, but it felt as though a huge weight was crushing her chest. Finally, she managed to speak. "Leo, Leo!" She gasped, breathlessly.

Leo appeared at the doorway.

"That definitely wasn't there earlier," Allissa said, pointing at a note on the kitchen counter. She scanned the room, checking to see that nothing else had changed.

They huddled together and read the spidery handwriting.

Ali's Fish Stall, Grand Bazaar, 3pm tomorrow.

31

BURAK TAPPED TWICE on the door. The small brass sign — *E.Kartan CEO* — vibrated aggressively. He looked around, checking for interested onlookers. The rest of the floor was empty. The other members of the executive team had been told to work from home for the next few days.

Working from home — that was a joke, Burak thought. That bunch of layabouts wouldn't know work if it slapped them in the face.

"Come in," came Esin's raised voice through the wood.

Burak pushed open the door, stepped inside, and closed it again.

Esin looked up at him from behind her computer. Bright midday light streamed through the window behind her. In the distance, the watery vein of the Golden Horn glittered amid the jumbled buildings of the city. From somewhere nearby, the first note of the Dhuhr — the midday muezzin, or call to prayer — sounded from a mosque. Dozens of others would soon join it in every neighbourhood in Istanbul and across the Islamic world.

"We may have a problem," Burak said, stepping forward, his voice barely above a whisper.

"Oh?" Esin said, tilting her head to one side.

"Yes, it's the Gerçeğin Koruyucuları."

"The Guardians of Truth," Esin spat.

Burak nodded.

"We've been watching them, as you instructed. They've made a few small claims, but nothing that anyone's paid much attention to."

"Nothing to worry about, then."

"Well, last night they contacted some investigators from England. I've looked into the pair, Leo Keane and Allissa Stockwell. They've got quite a form for this sort of thing. Remember the scandal with the Latvian government a few months ago..."

Esin thought about it and nodded. Half the government, including the favourite to be the next president, had been forced to resign when some secret papers were brought to light.

"Well. We don't yet know who sent them here," Burak continued. "It might be one of the British newspapers, or maybe they're just poking their noses in —"

"Do you know where they are?" Esin interrupted.

"I can find out." Burak nodded. "We have contacts all over the city."

"Then we need to get rid of them," Esin said. "Today."

32

Leo watched a couple in the window of a café sip at their coffees while poking at their phones. The pair had exchanged less than a dozen words in the time Leo and Allissa had been there.

Leo sighed and glanced up at the golden hands of the clock on the wall — quarter to three.

He dug out the note which they'd found last night in their apartment and smoothed it out on the table. There was something sinister about the spidery handwriting in the daylight.

Somewhere behind the counter, a dishwasher chugged. A radio played tinny pop music. The barista swatted at a fly with a discoloured dishtowel.

"What're you worried about?" Allissa asked, watching him from above the rim of her second drink.

"I... Well... I don't... I'm not sure." Leo rubbed his hands together and willed away the familiar claws of anxiety. It was a feeling he knew well now, one that he claimed to control, but was never totally sure.

"Yeah. How someone knew where we're staying..." Allissa said, trailing off. She didn't want to antagonise Leo's anxiety after yesterday's events at the Hagia Sophia. In the time they'd known each other, Allissa had seen Leo act with bravery and lucidity in situations that would render other people petrified. Yet, she'd also seen him unable to leave the house for days on end for no discernible reason. Fortunately, it rarely got that bad.

Leo rubbed his hands together again, the tendons in his wrists and forearms bulging.

"It's time to go, anyway," she said, glancing up at the clock on the wall. "We need to find Ali's fish store by three."

Leo nodded, cleared his throat, and stood.

They clattered through the door of the café and into the bright afternoon sunlight. The entrance to the Grand Bazaar sat across a small square. Gold letters in both Arabic and English glimmered from a red arch. The noises of traffic jibed with bubbling conversation.

"Don't you think we should have sorted out some kind of back-up plan?" Leo asked, his eyes frantically roaming the square. A large woman in a bright blue headscarf pushed a trolly stacked with boxes towards the main entrance. A man, thick forearms straining under the weight of two carrier bags, struggled in the direction of a bus stop.

"Like what?" Allissa said, more sharply than she'd intended. She glanced up at Leo and then linked her arm through his. "Honestly, it'll be fine. It's the middle of the day in one of the city's busiest places. Plus, this place has security guards, cameras, all that sort of thing." Allissa glanced at a man in a light brown security uniform smoking beside the entrance. She had to admit he didn't look like a particularly dynamic force. She thought better than bringing that up to Leo.

They stepped through the entrance and into the Grand Bazaar.

"It will be f —" Allissa's words cut short as the Bazaar came into sight. Having visited markets, souks and bazaars all across the world, Allissa didn't think the Grand Bazaar would be anything new. Yet, it was. Ornate tiles covering the vaulted ceiling shone under bright lights — blues, and yellows, and mauves. Raised voices of negotiation reverberated, each fighting for the next sale. The wares of the sellers lined up like a colourful army ready for attack. Turkish flags hung proud in the still air.

Leo and Allissa wandered forward, eyes scanning the fabrics and shawls in multitudes of colours and shades. They walked a hundred yards, ignoring the frantic shouts from merchants. "Just look, you will love. For the lady!"

After two hundred yards, the great hall opened into a crossroads. Leo and Allissa paused. Rows of stalls fanned out as far as they could see in both directions.

Allissa glanced at the time on her phone. "We've got ten minutes," she said. "We're going to need some help."

A young woman in a bright red shawl appeared from a nearby stall. The folds of the material swayed around her knees. "You need shawl, beautiful fabrics, just try," she crowed the call of the merchants, smiling brightly.

"No," Allissa said, turning abruptly. Looking into the woman's impossibly large caramel-coloured eyes, Allissa softened her tone. "But we do need your help with something."

The woman listened intently. A moment later she curled her finger, motioning Leo and Allissa to follow, then turned on her heels and strode off with surprising speed into the market.

"This way," Allissa said, gesturing to Leo. Leo shrugged

and followed. He glanced ahead. He could only just make out the woman in the red shawl as she deftly navigated the crowded market, folding a shoulder, twisting her torso, and pushing her way through.

They turned a corner and rushed past rows of beautiful pottery — Allissa craned her neck, glimpsing ornately painted patterns of blue and gold. They reached another T-junction. Two more market halls spanned out to the right and left. Leo glanced from one way to the other before seeing the red shawl turning a corner ahead.

"That way," he shouted to Allissa, trainers squeaking over the tiled floor as they picked up speed. Leo swung around a corner, with Allissa on his heels. Leo leapt to the right to avoid colliding with two women pushing buggies.

The woman with the red shawl was just ten feet ahead now. Leo glanced at the stalls, which in this section of the bazaar sold pots, pans and other home wares. There was no way they would have found this particular stall on their own.

The woman in the shawl turned to the right up ahead. A few seconds later, Leo and Allissa followed. Cold air moved through the bazaar now. Leo and Allissa rushed past large displays of meat. Half carcasses lay on slabs of wood. Burly men in blood-stained aprons arranged cuts of meat on beds of ice. Leo almost lost sight of the woman. A flash of red, turning the corner ahead, indicated the way.

They powered on, narrowly avoiding a man carrying several plucked chickens by the feet. Leo turned the corner and stopped suddenly. Allissa almost ran into the back of him. The woman stood in front of them, a broad smile on her face.

"Ali's is there," she said, pointing to one of the dozen or

more fish stalls. "You can't miss him. Man with the beard." The woman's hands cupped her chin to indicate the beard.

"Thank you," Allissa said, rummaging through her pockets. "Let me give you something —"

"No need," the woman interrupted, placing her hand on Allissa's arm. "We're all here to help each other." And with that, she was gone, sashaying back through the hordes of people.

Leo turned, but the red glint of the shawl had already disappeared.

"We've got two minutes," Allissa said, checking the time.

The pair rushed up the hall, looking for a man with a beard.

Sure enough, three stalls up on the right side, a fishmonger with a giant beard dextrously gutted a fish on a slab. Leo and Allissa stopped and examined the man. His dark eyes focused on the knife in his hands, quickly slicing through the flesh.

Leo and Allissa stepped forward, out of the flow of people. Leo glanced around, his heart rhythmically pounding in his chest. The sounds of negotiation and tapping feet pattered from the ceiling tiles. The shrill ringing of a phone pierced the hubbub. Leo and Allissa both ignored the noise, not recognising the ring tone.

"I guess we wait, " Leo said, answering Allissa's unasked question.

The shrill ringing of the phone continued. It was coming from somewhere nearby. People flowed up and down the hall.

"Hey," came a thick accented voice. "You not going to answer that?"

Leo and Allissa looked up, almost in surprise. The

heavy-set fishmonger considered them. He pointed at the counter beside Leo and Allissa with a blood-stained fish knife. Leo and Allissa glanced down. A mobile phone glowed, ringing noisily.

33

"Gentlemen, you look fantastic," Esin said as she walked into the conference room.

Three men stopped talking and turned to face her. A world away from the normal weak men that occupied this room, these guys were tough, imposing and downright scary.

Esin examined each of them in turn. Muscles bulged beneath their black uniforms. Burak stood in the centre, flanked by his most trusted colleagues.

Esin nodded slowly. Just looking at these men was enough to encourage anyone to get out of their way.

Burak pulled on his jacket. The other men did the same.

"Perfect," Esin said, looking from the word 'POLIS' printed on the back of the jacket to the crest of the National Police on the chest. "You look... well, very convincing," she said.

Burak pushed a black cap down over his head. The other men copied.

"Everything else is in order? You have the transport and something to make sure they don't bother us again?"

Burak nodded. "Yes, everything is in order."

"Excellent," Esin said, touching Burak on the shoulder. "Get down there and get rid of them."

34

The phone was a basic, low-tech model — a burner. A long and mysterious number scrolled across the yellow display.

The volume of the market rose. Two women, swinging string bags and talking loudly, pushed past. The knife of the butcher, two stalls up, thudded into the chopping block, cracking bones and slicing flesh.

The phone trilled again. It was the sort of noise modern phones don't have. A bleeping electronic howl, never found in the natural world.

"Answer it," the fishmonger barked, scowling, his knife paused mid slice. The body of a great silver fish lay gutless beneath his left paw.

Leo snatched up the phone and glanced left and right. Was somebody watching them? Clearly thinking the same thing, Allissa's eyes darted about. The bustling market was unchanged. No one paid them any attention.

The phone trilled once more.

Leo thumbed the green button, held it to his ear, and locked eyes with Allissa.

"You must listen to me very carefully." A male, accented

voice streamed through the speaker. Leo focused on the voice, cutting out the sounds of the market. "I'm afraid I have no time to explain, but you must trust me. You are in great danger."

Whilst the voice was accented, the man spoke English with the confidence of many years' practice.

Leo didn't reply. A burst of noise echoed from the vaulted ceiling. A cry of raised voices. The thump of boots on tiles.

Allissa looked towards the sound. Nothing appeared to be out of place yet.

"There are people coming for you. I can get you out of there, but you must do exactly as I say."

"Wait, what?" Leo said. "Who's coming for us? Why are —"

Allissa glanced from the raised hubbub to Leo. Colour drained from her expression.

"Ninety seconds ago, a group of men entered the Grand Bazaar by the north gate," the man said. "They are dressed as National Police, but they are not the police. In twenty seconds, they will turn the corner and head your way."

Another cry reverberated down the hallway. Someone shrieked, followed by the sound of shattering pottery. The roar of thundering boots was clearly audible now.

"Listen," Leo said, "I don't know who you are, or what's going on, but —" he paused, catching sight of Allissa. She stared wide eyed towards the incoming noise. The sound of each boot was distinct now. People scurried out of the way. Leo removed the phone from his ear and listened. Raised voices shouted commands.

Leo's hand tightened around the phone, his knuckles losing colour. He tried to swallow. Gravel lodged in his throat. He lifted the phone back to his ear.

"Okay," Leo said, his voice grave. "What's going on?"

"I have no time to explain now," the man said. "When you are in safety, I will tell you everything. For now, I need you to do exactly what I say."

"Okay." Leo grasped Allissa's arm with his free hand. "We're listening."

35

"Turn right and run as fast as you can to the end of the hall," the man explained. "Then left at the T-junction."

The incoming sounds were closer now. Boots thundered against the tiles. Shoppers, pushed from the path of the pursuers, yelled and howled.

Leo grasped Allissa's arm and pulled them to the right. They darted past a family gathered around a fish stall. Leo's trainers squeaked across the tiles as they picked up pace. Leo let go of Allissa's arm and the pair separated to avoid an old man with a walking stick. Leo leapt over a box and kept running. They reached the end of the hall.

"Turn left," Leo shouted, powering around the corner.

Allissa followed a moment later.

This corridor was quieter. No stalls flanked the sides. Storage boxes and trolleys littered the walls. The passage rose towards a bright circle of afternoon sunlight.

Leo clamped the phone against his ear.

"Good, you're doing well," the man said. It was clear and crisp. "Once you're outside, you need to —"

"No, wait," Leo shouted breathlessly.

"What?"

"The gate," Leo panted. "Someone's closing the gate."

Up ahead, a silhouetted figure pulled a metal gate across the entrance. It clanged shut.

Leo and Allissa reached the bars, panting. They were just a few seconds too late, but the figure had already disappeared into a crowd of people.

Allissa pushed the gate as hard as she could. The steel bars shook, but wouldn't move.

Thumping feet echoed up the passage. A deep male voice shouted commands.

"It's locked," Leo said. "What now?"

"Wait one moment." A keyboard rattled.

"Stop where you are!" A voice reverberated up the passage. The footsteps crunched into silence.

Leo and Allissa turned slowly.

"There is no point running. We have you surrounded." A man, grey eyes burning above a grim smile, watched them closely. Two other men, muscular and imposing, stood behind him. If they had weapons, they hadn't drawn them yet. Their presence was daunting enough.

Leo's Adam's apple bobbed uselessly in his throat. *This is becoming a bit of a habit,* Leo thought. *Too much of a habit.*

Leo glanced at Allissa. From her expression, he assumed she was thinking the same. Leo kept the phone clamped to his ear.

The men took a step forward. The normal babble of the market streamed down the hallway. Leo glanced through the locked bars of the gate behind them. People meandered in the sunshine down towards the Golden Horn.

"Okay, I've got it. It's a tricky one, but I can still get you out." The man on the phone sounded urgent now.

"I'm listening," Leo said between deep breaths. His pulse raced at the thought.

"Put the phone down," the muscular man barked. He moved slowly, reaching for the gun holstered at his hip.

Dressed as National Police — Leo remembered — no one would question these men carrying arms.

"There's a door on your right, five meters away," said the man on the phone. "When I tell you, go through there. It shouldn't be locked. Wait for my signal."

Leo saw the door and then looked back at the man. He hadn't noticed the door on the way past. Painted the same colour as the wall, it was easy to miss.

The muscular man's grin widened. His hand hovered above his hip.

"These men have guns," Leo hissed into the phone.

"Don't worry, they won't shoot you here," came the reply. "Not in this public place."

The man's gloved hand moved closer to his firearm.

"I'm not going to ask what makes you so sure," Leo whispered.

"Just trust me." The man on the phone sounded oddly cheerful now. "Go through that door and then up the staircase to the left. Wait for my signal, okay?"

"I'm losing patience now." The big man howled. "Put the phone down and step this way."

"Just a few more seconds," the man hissed down the phone line.

Leo whispered the instructions to Allissa. She nodded in reply.

The big man sneered. "No one needs to get hurt —"

An almighty crash boomed from the hall behind the men. It reverberated several times throughout the market. A flurry of cries and shrieks followed. The men glanced towards it.

"Go, now!" shouted the man on the phone.

Leo leapt towards the door, his feet sliding across the tiles. He covered the distance in three paces and crashed through. The door swung open and slammed against the wall. Allissa followed him a moment later.

The shouts of surprise died away and the voices of the men rose.

Leo glanced around the space. A big freezer consumed one wall of the small room. Cobweb covered crates languished against the other.

Allissa slammed the door shut.

"Great, up the stairs to your left," prompted the man on the phone.

Leo spun around and saw a narrow staircase leading up behind the row of boxes.

"This way." Leo indicated the stairs.

"No wait, help me with this." Allissa jumped over to the freezer and shoved it as hard as she could. The appliance barely moved. Leo jumped toward it and together they heaved it up onto one edge. A final shove sent the thing crashing against the door. Dust billowed up in a great cloud.

The handle twisted, and the door opened an inch and then stopped. One man shoved the door with his shoulder. It crunched into the freezer but wouldn't open. Loud voices streamed through the gap.

"Come on," Leo shouted, pulling Allissa towards the staircase. "That won't hold them for long."

The door creaked and shattered behind them. Hinges screeched.

Leo and Allissa charged up the staircase, through another

door, and into a narrow passageway. Leo peered through one of several small arches cut into the wall. Several feet below, normal service had resumed in the market hall. People milled about the stalls, and merchants touted for business.

"Fifty metres ahead, climb the steel staircase."

Leo relayed the instructions to Allissa, shouting above the noise of the market.

"How does he know this?" she shouted back.

"No idea." Leo's trainers slid to a stop, sending a cloud of dust into the air.

"I can't see a staircase," he barked into the phone.

Light streamed in thick bars through high windows. Dust shot through the bars like comets.

The noise of a tapping keyboard came down the phone line. "It's there. On the right," said the man.

"There," Allissa stated.

Leo turned around and looked again slowly. As his eyes adjusted to the light, he was astonished to see a thin, rusty spiral staircase extending vertically from behind a pile of dusty boxes. A layer of crusted dust rendered it barely visible against the stone.

Leo pulled the boxes aside and grabbed a rung. He shook the structure. The metal clanged and wobbled. Leo peered tentatively upwards. Thirty feet above, the staircase disappeared into the ceiling.

A crash echoed up the corridor, followed by the raised voices of the men.

"The men have passed the door." The man took on a serious tone now. "You must climb the staircase."

"Up we go," Leo said, thudding up the first two steps. The metal clunked and groaned under his feet. The staircase wobbled dangerously, leaning away from the supporting wall. Leo glanced down to check Allissa was following. She was a few steps behind him, her mouth set into a frown of concentration.

Leo climbed as quickly as he could around the tight spiral. After a minute, he glanced back down at the floor beneath them. They'd climbed at least twenty feet. The wobbling was even more pronounced at this height, moving this way and that. Looking out at the room, Leo slipped on the thin tread. A clang jarred from the structure. His knee struck the rung and a white-hot pain pounded through his leg. The staircase swayed further away from the supporting wall.

Leo grasped the phone tighter to stop it slipping from his hand. He glanced down at the ground between the treads, then instantly regretted it. The room wobbled and swayed.

The voices of the men and the pounding feet drew closer.

Leo pulled a deep breath. His heart thudded like a jackhammer against his ribs. He struggled back onto his feet and slowly, painstakingly, continued to climb.

Several steps later, Leo climbed through the ceiling itself. Dust lay thick on the rungs here and with each step a great cloud of it billowed into the air. Walls of brick enclosed the staircase on all sides.

Allissa crouched and glanced into the space behind them. The men emerged from the doorway below and ran along the passage. Their raised voices and footsteps filled the room.

Leo forced himself up the final few stairs, every instinct wanting to give up and return to solid ground. Then he came to a horizontal hatch blocking their passage. He pushed his shoulder into it. The hatch shuddered but didn't move.

"What now?" Leo hissed into the phone.

"That hatch hasn't been opened in over a decade. A strong shoulder should do it," said the man, as though it were the most obvious thing in the world.

Leo barged it again. The man was right. The thing didn't seem secure.

"But wait," the man hissed urgently.

"Why —"

"The men," Allissa interrupted. "They haven't realised we're here."

36

"Harder, get it open!" Burak barked at his men. He glanced around. Noise from the bazaar drifted up the passage towards them. That was a good sign. No one thought their appearance was unusual.

The men charged against the flimsy door. The wood cracked but didn't move. They tried again. A cloud of dust rose around them.

"They've wedged it with something."

"Keep trying," Burak growled.

The men turned back and struck at the door again. Finally, after two more thumps, the door split and tumbled inwards. The men yanked the shards of wood out of the way, revealing a freezer lying on its side.

Burak swore under his breath and forced a clenched fist into the palm of the other hand. These two were going to pay.

The men dropped the shards of broken door and scrambled over the freezer. Shattered wood covered the room inside and dust filled the air.

Burak glanced at the boxes piled against the walls.

"This way, boss," shouted one of the men. In a shady corner of the room, a narrow metal staircase led up into the ceiling.

"After them," Burak grumbled through a sneer.

37

Leo froze, listening to the thumping feet and the gruff voices below.

"Wait," the man on the phone said again. "They'll pass in a minute."

Leo tried to pull a breath, but it only partly entered his chest before his anxiety forced it away. He tried again. A snatch of air slipped into his lungs. A vice gripped his chest. His muscles tensed.

Leo looked around for something to ease the spiral of his anxiety. Experience had taught him that if he could concentrate on something good at times like this, then he had a chance of maintaining control. He looked around. His eyes roamed from the walls to the dirty steel staircase. Nothing gave him the solace he needed.

"I think they've passed," Allissa whispered. "Leo." She tapped him on the side of the leg.

Leo turned, twisted into the staircase, and looked at Allissa. He took a breath. A nourishing lungful of air filled his chest.

"Go now, as quietly as you can," the man said again.

"Okay," Leo said, turning to face the hatch on the narrow staircase. He passed the phone to Allissa and climbed until his shoulder rested against the wood.

"Now," Allissa said, repeating the man's instructions.

Leo did as he was told. He crouched down and then slammed his shoulder into the wood. The staircase clanged, and the wood splintered.

"Again," Allissa hissed.

Leo repeated the motion. The hatch moved an inch but settled back into position. "I think I'll get it this time."

Leo pulled back even further. He tightened his hands around the spine of the staircase and bedded his feet into the rungs. He tensed his muscles. His face contorted into a scowl. Then, exhaling, he slammed into the hatch with all the strength he could muster. The wood screeched, splintered, and shot open. Leo shot forward, losing his grip on the staircase. The hatch fell to one side.

Leo peered out and saw the roof of the Grand Bazaar and a dome of blue sky above. Then gravity came to work, forcing him down towards the staircase. He scrambled for a handhold, fingers slipping across the tiles. Sharp metal clawed against his shins and thighs. He lashed out, grabbing for anything that could arrest his fall.

Allissa saw him coming. She gripped the steel with her free hand, but not quickly enough. Leo's body slammed into hers, sending her backwards down the stairs and knocking the phone from her grasp. She reached out frantically as the stairs slipped beneath her. Eventually, she caught hold of a rung and pulled them both to a stop.

Leo rested on his elbows for a moment. His legs and arms ached. He didn't dare look down at the hard floor, a deadly distance below.

Leo scrambled back up the stairs and out onto the roof.

He was dizzy, disorientated and longed for something solid beneath his feet.

Allissa scrambled out, and stood beside Leo on a lower section of the bazaar's expansive roof. The serpentine curves of the tiled roofs stretched out before them. In the distance, the very tips of domes and minarets pierced the skyline. To the left, another staircase led up onto the great curving roof of the bazaar.

"What now?" Leo said, forcing himself to cough.

"I don't know," Allissa replied. "The phone. It's down there."

Leo looked from the skyline to Allissa, and then back down the hatch.

"We need that phone," Allissa said. "We've no idea which way to go without it."

Leo nodded. "I'll go back."

"No." Allissa grabbed his arm. "I will. My balance is better than yours, plus I dropped it."

Leo nodded, relieved. "Okay. Be careful."

38

BURAK LED his men up the small staircase and into another, larger room. He glanced through a small window in the left wall. The market's hubbub continued below. He examined the window. It was too small to climb through, plus there was a twenty-foot drop into the market hall below. He ran on.

The passage was long and thin, with boxes and crates stacked on both sides. Burak slowed to pick his way past an overflowing pile of detritus. Ahead, the passage turned to the right. Burak swore under his breath - there was no knowing how many hidden rooms and passages this building contained.

Burak reached the bend in the passage and paused. The man following close behind him almost ran him over. A narrow opening led off to the left here. The floor and the piles of boxes were covered in a thick layer of dust and grime. Burak examined it closely. It was difficult to make out anything. He pulled a torch from his pocket. Moving the beam across the dust, no footprints were visible.

"They're in here somewhere," Burak said, turning to face his men.

At that moment, he noticed something. His eyes widened as he recognised the movement. Thirty feet above them, the girl scurried down a narrow staircase, grabbed something, and then rushed back up onto the roof.

39

Allissa leapt from the hatch less than two minutes later, the phone held high. Relief washed over Leo. He took the phone and held it to his ear.

"There you are," the man said cheerfully. "Now, take that staircase behind you."

"No, wait," Leo said, frustration boiling over. "We've outrun those men. Now tell us who you are and how you know what's going on."

"Look up."

Leo squinted against the sun. He couldn't see anything at first, then slowly, a tiny shape came into view. He heard the soft hum of electric motors. A drone hovered twenty feet above the roof.

"I also have access to the security cameras inside. As for who I am, I'll explain that when we meet."

"When will that be?" Leo demanded.

"Soon," the man said. "But right now, you're going to have to run again. The men have seen you and are climbing the staircase."

The clang of footsteps on the metal stairs drifted above

the murmur of the city. Allissa ran over to the hatch and peered inside.

"They're coming." She looked up at Leo. "What now?"

Leo turned and charged up the staircase. The structure was nothing more than a series of rungs bolted to the bazaar's ancient tiles. At the summit, a row of boards ran in both directions.

Leo reached the top and looked from right to left. The city spanned out before him like an oil painting. The curving roof of the market rose and fell in great swathes of tile and tin. The domes and minarets of the city's countless mosques punctuated the horizon, and in the distance the stretch of water — the Bosphorus — at which Europe stops and Asia begins, shone like a bed of diamonds in the afternoon sun. The only thing to suggest this was not an antique oil painting were the satellite dishes and air conditioning units, which hummed and ticked in the afternoon breeze.

"Turn right," the man said. Leo glanced above him. He couldn't see the drone now against the bright sky.

Leo stepped tentatively from the top of the steps and onto the boards. He took a deep breath. The scent of spices and fresh coffee had now been replaced with the fug of car fumes and the distant taste of the ocean.

Allissa reached the apex and stood beside him. "Where now?"

Leo removed the phone from his ear and held it against his chest. He glanced towards the approaching sound of their pursuers and then turned to face Allissa. Istanbul fanned out behind her. The ethereal curves of the Blue Mosque, the imposing shape of the Hagia Sophia, and the waters of the Bosphorus, all shimmered like a dream. Thousands of years of secrets, lies and conflict at the confluence of continents.

Somewhere far below, a motorbike started up and revved away. A ship, cruising its way south, sounded its horn.

Leo's heart thudded steadily against his rib cage.

Leo pointed right. Allissa looked at him, smiled, and then set off at a run down the walkway.

A gust of wind whipped around him. Leo glanced back at the hatch and then set off after Allissa.

His feet thudding over the boards, Leo caught up with Allissa quickly. The roof curved down before them, hemmed in by a series of boxy concrete buildings. Leo tried not to look at the steep angle of the roofs or imagine the pain and injury that falling could cause.

A flock of doves enjoying the shelter of a rusting air-conditioner fluttered and cooed into the air.

The far end of the market came into view. Allissa slowed to a jog and then stopped. She peered down over the edge. Forty feet below, a narrow alleyway ran down the side of the building. The wall of the next building loomed up ten feet away.

Allissa pulled away from the edge; looking over the precipice without a barrier made her dizzy.

"No, don't!" Allissa instinctively put an arm out to block Leo. He stopped, inches from the edge, and reeled back, throwing a hand to his chest.

The sound of raised voices drifted towards them. Leo and Allissa turned around. The men stomped down the walkway towards them.

"What now?" Leo barked into the phone. "You've got us up here. You must have a pretty good plan!"

"Of course," the man replied calmly. "Slide down the roof to your left and up onto the next apex."

Leo examined the roofs to their left. Sure enough, they

connected at the bottom in the centre. He glanced back at the men, who were now just fifty feet behind. The leading man's face distorted into a mask of exertion and anger.

Leo scrambled from the walkway and down onto the tiles. Terracotta clattered beneath his feet. He leaned over and grabbed the boards with his free hand.

"Quickly, now!" the man hissed.

Leo let go and half ran, half tumbled down the roof. Delicate tiles cracked and skittered beneath his trainers. Fragments slid down the roof. Leo reached out and steadied himself. He was now ten feet below the apex, and the gradient had lessened. He listened for a moment. Boots thundered nearby.

"This plan had better be good," he mumbled beneath his breath.

He slid to the roof's lowest point and leapt over a small drainage gulley, then scrambled up the opposite side. His feet slipped over the tiles several times, sending shards and dust careering downwards. He grabbed hold of the apex of the parallel roof and hauled himself up.

Allissa watched Leo with her hands on her hips. She glanced back at the men, now less than thirty feet away. She cocked her head to the side and jumped. Landing nimbly on the balls of her feet, she ran across roofs and leapt across the gully. Then, with the grace of a gymnast, she caught the uppermost tiles of the parallel roof, and with one swift move, swung her leg over.

"Show off," Leo said, catching her eye and failing to quell a smile. He held the phone to his ear. "Now what?"

"Walk to the end of the roof," the man commanded. "There, across the alleyway, just over six feet away, you'll see another rooftop."

Leo struggled to his feet and did what he was told. The

boards on the summit of this rooftop appeared thinner and less secure than the last. Leo saw the roof that the unknown voice had indicated. He peered off the edge. The passage was narrow, but the drop was still disconcertingly far.

A strong breeze whipped in from the Bosphorus, slapping Leo around the face. Leo wobbled. He shot his arms out in an effort to steady himself. He tentatively moved the phone to his ear again.

"Get a good run up," the man said, "and jump onto that rooftop."

The meaning of the man's words sunk in slowly.

Get a good run up and jump onto that rooftop.

Jump across a six-foot gap, over a forty-foot drop.

Leo removed the phone from his ear and looked directly at Allissa.

"The guy wants us to jump." His face drained of colour.

Allissa scampered across to the edge and peered down. Her knuckles closed around the tiles, whitening with the pressure. A flurry of debris drifted down the alleyway several stories below. A cat, its fur bedraggled and patchy, ran between bins.

"No, we can't, it's too —"

"Listen," the man said. "Considering your running speed and the drop in height between the roofs, you can do it. I know you can."

"What about the —" Leo peered down the precipice.

Behind them, three pairs of boots skidded to a stop.

"There are two ways out of this," the man explained calmly. "One is to do what I say. The other is to try your luck with those gun wielding men."

40

Esin stared through her office window, watching a tanker slide up the gently lapping waters of the Bosphorus. The boat looked calm and serene against the chaos of the city.

She turned and peered in the direction of the Grand Bazaar. From the office she couldn't quite see the antique roofs of the world-famous market, but knew it was nearby.

She imagined Burak and his men storming through the building and dragging those two interfering detectives kicking and screaming out of the bazaar.

Those amateurs could go right back to where they came from. This city was no place for them.

Esin spun on her heels and scrutinized the picture of Sadik-Tech's last CEO. Esin told everyone that she kept the photograph on the wall to remind them of what the company stood for. Ahmed Sadik had been a very ethical man — too ethical by half, in Esin's opinion.

Her eyes drifted across the picture now. She had no need to focus on it; the image was seared into her brain. In the photograph, the righteous idiot was laying the foundation stone of a new community centre — paid for by the company's generous donation. That was a hundred thousand lira they would never see again. A sizeable chunk of money. Esin could do with that cash now. "Fool!" she whispered sharply.

Esin tapped the desk impatiently, her long fingernails rattling against the wood. She forced a smile. Really, she knew the picture remained there to remind her that you had to do exactly what was necessary to succeed. Sometimes that was hard, sometimes it was dangerous, sometimes illegal — either way, it had to be done.

Wasting bags of cash had no place in her idea of running the company.

Memories of that snowy night up in the mountains spooled through her mind. The look of shock on Sadik's face had been priceless. The man had not even considered her to be a danger. A sweet woman like her — he wouldn't have seen it coming in a thousand years.

Esin looked back out at the city through the window. That night up in the mountains was the event that had set them on this course. Esin had stepped up. She had proved to everyone — the stuffy men on the board, the shareholders, to Sadik and herself — that she was not afraid to take decisive and lethal action.

She glanced down at her fingernails. The detectives should be in Burak's custody now. Esin's *decisive* and *lethal* action would soon see them out of the way, too. After that, it would be time to move on to the next stage of the plan. This was the most daring plan of her career. The stakes and rewards were higher than ever. It had to work.

Esin glanced back at the picture. She would do anything she could to make it work. She wouldn't allow anyone to get in the way.

A knock resounded from the office door.

"Yes?" Esin shouted.

The mechanism clicked and the door swung open. A wide-bodied man came into view. His sandy hair was closely cropped, and his thick neck strained against his shirt's collar.

"Mr Fasslane," Esin said, steepling her fingers. "I trust you are as comfortable as can be in your makeshift home."

"You call that comfortable?" Fasslane spat. "I'm basically a prisoner in this place. I'm the most famous person in the world —"

"It won't be for long, Mr Fasslane. In fact, I wanted to tell you that as long as we get our minor problem solved, then we should be able to move out tonight."

Fasslane scowled, his jowls wobbling. "About time."

41

Allissa slammed against the inside wall of the windowless truck as it turned a corner. Her shoulder bounced against Leo, sitting on the bench beside her. Allissa didn't know where they were going, but it didn't look good.

It was dark inside the truck. The only light seeped from a dulled bulkhead lamp on the ceiling. Strange, dark patches bloomed across the floor. Allissa tried not to think too closely about what they might be.

A man slumped into the seat opposite them, his large frame twisted uncomfortably in the truck's cramped interior. His dark eyes moved from Leo to Allissa and then back again. His lips parted into a smirk, showing two missing teeth.

Allissa considered the events of the last ten minutes. Up there on the rickety rooftop, the jump had felt impossible.

The truck turned again. Allissa's head banged against the side. Maybe they should have risked injury or even death to give it a go. But then, even if they had successfully made the jump — which hadn't seemed likely at the time — the men could still have opened fire.

The truck screeched around a corner and picked up speed.

Allissa focused on the turns they made, hoping it would give her some clue where they were being taken. The truck barrelled slightly to the right, or was it the left?

Allissa couldn't even calculate how long they'd been inside the van. Allissa stared at the man sat opposite. Muscles bulged beneath his clothes.

"Lovely ride, this," Allissa said, catching the man's gaze. He scowled and looked away. "First class hospitality. Can I leave a review online?"

Leo huffed beside her.

"Keep quiet," the man snarled.

Allissa smiled sweetly, trying to dispel her blooming sense of worry.

She glanced at Leo beside her. Outwardly, he looked calm, although she knew him better than that. She reached across and rubbed his knee in a gesture that said; *we'll be fine.*

He nodded; *I know we will.*

The truck slowed, turned a series of tight corners, and then squealed to a stop. The engine idled.

Footsteps approached the vehicle. Leo's body stiffened.

One voice spoke, and another answered. Instructions were given in a guttural language Allissa didn't understand. Was it Turkish?

Then the truck crawled forward again.

Another vehicle passed. The deep growl of its hefty engine groaned beyond the truck's sides. They heard another noise, too. A distant hiss and whistle. It sounded mechanical. Allissa couldn't place it above the truck's engine roar. She glanced at Leo.

Leo shrugged and shook his head.

The truck rumbled on for a few minutes before pulling to a stop. This time, the engine coughed into silence. Allissa tilted her head and listened closely for any sound that might indicate their location.

Nothing.

One of the cab doors clunked open, then boots thundered to the floor and strode towards the rear of the truck. The rear door clicked as it swung open. Light streamed into the vehicle. Allissa looked towards it, her eyes stinging. A man's bulky silhouette filled the space.

The man at the door barked instructions, and the sitting man staggered to his feet and shuffled out. The man at the door climbed in and slid onto the bench. He slammed the door, and the light faded.

Allissa looked at him closely for the first time. He looked like the classic thug they'd come up against time and time again. The black uniform of the National Police barely concealed his thick arms and muscular chest. His clean-shaven skin was so weathered it looked like bark. A thick scar ran down the side of his face, twisting his lips into a constant sneer. His grey eyes roamed from Allissa, to Leo, then back again.

"Well, I'm glad that fun is now over." He pushed his knuckles together until his fingers clicked.

Allissa rolled her eyes. *Could this guy be any more of a cliché?*

"What do you want?" Leo said.

He's doing a good job at appearing confident, Allissa thought.

The man laughed. "Straight to the point. I like this guy." He pointed a thick finger at Leo. "Istanbul is a wonderful city, don't you think?" He looked down at his hands and then up at the detectives again. "You can get a beer, get a shag, hey, even smoke a bit of hashish if you want — whatever you feel like doing. I don't care. That is a lot of freedom, yes?"

"Who are you?" Allissa said.

"Now that is a good question, but not at the right time. Listen. For our citizens and our esteemed visitors to have all that choice, all that freedom, all that liberty, there has to be some lines that are not crossed. Some rules that are not broken. Otherwise, the system, it — boom." The man made the gesture of an explosion with his fingers.

"I understand," Allissa said, nodding. Leo rolled his eyes.

"Oh, good, good." The man smiled.

"I understand that you're wasting our time. Get to the point, or take me to the nearest bar. Your hospitality stinks."

The man laughed again. He rubbed his right fist in the palm of his left hand. "Okay, okay, I can see you are a... *sharp cookie*. I'll get to the point. We know you are here on tourist visas —" the man slid his hand into his jacket pocket and pulled out two British passports. Allissa recognised them immediately.

"Hey, how did you get —"

The man raised the palm of his hand to silence the interruption.

"We also know that you are poking around in things that do not concern you. These things concern the freedom of the Turkish people."

"Rubbish," Leo muttered.

"We also know that today you have been in contact with a known terrorist. A man who is an enemy of the Turkish state."

"I have no idea what you're talking about." Allissa shook her head.

The man removed a small audio player from his pocket.

He poked a button. A few seconds of the conversation between Leo and the man on the phone filled the back of the truck.

"You have nothing to say about this? The man you are speaking to calls himself *'The Guardian of Truth'*. He has been a blight on this country for many years. He has caused protests, violence and even assassinations. Now, you seem like good people, but you're mixed up in something very bad here."

The man examined Leo and Allissa closely.

"I can see in your country you are somewhat minor celebrities for these sorts of *shenanigans*. Let me tell you, though, this is not welcome here in Istanbul."

The man banged on the side of the van. The door creaked open. Light flooded in. He gave some instructions, and an envelope was passed inside. He flipped open the envelope and passed a sheet of paper to Leo and Allissa.

"You have seats on the next flight back to London. It leaves in just over an hour."

Allissa glanced at the paper. It was a boarding pass for a British Airways flight to London Heathrow.

"You get on that plane, and I will never see you again," the man said, leaning forward and examining Leo and Allissa myopically. "If I do see you again, be warned that the Turkish justice system is harsh, particularly for terrorists." He shouted another instruction. Leo and Allissa's rucksacks were pushed into the truck.

"Now get out. Now!" the man shouted.

They glanced at each other, picked up their bags and stepped unsteadily out of the truck. Allissa blinked while her eyes adjusted to the harsh sunlight.

A great glass wall reared up before them. Allissa spun

around and saw, in the distance, the giant tail fin of an aeroplane.

Their bags slung over their shoulder, the men pushed Leo and Allissa through a set of double doors and bundled them up a flight of stairs. Through another set of doors, Leo and Allissa were shoved into the departure lounge of Istanbul Ataturk Airport.

Allissa recognised the sound she'd heard some minutes before — a jet engine at take-off.

42

Leo and Allissa blinked hard beneath the bright lights of the airport. The place was strange and foreign.

They staggered through a group of passengers queuing for departure.

Leo glanced at the screen at the front of the line — *Amsterdam*.

Disorientated, he knocked the shoulder of a young woman coming the other way.

"Sorry, sorry," he muttered, glancing over his shoulder. The woman had already weaved into the crowd.

Allissa grabbed Leo's arm and led them to a quiet end of the departure lounge. A few passengers sprawled on chairs, reading books or scrolling through their phones. Through the window, an aeroplane lumbered soundlessly in the direction of the runway. A female voice spoke through unseen speakers, the words sterile and distant.

Leo glanced back in the direction from which they'd come. The line inched its way forward. Everything seemed normal.

Allissa dropped her bag to a row of aluminium seats.

"We need to stop and think for a moment." She paced up and down. "What's just happened? One moment we were on the roof of the Grand Bazaar and now we're here. What's going on?"

Leo dropped his bag next to Allissa's. He glanced around again. Two airport staff slid past on an electronic buggy.

"Wouldn't we normally have to go through security checks and that?" Leo asked. "I suppose the police can do what they want."

"If they *were* the police. I have no idea what to think now." Allissa's eyes met Leo's. "Didn't the guy on the phone say they were just dressed as the police?"

Leo nodded. "It's strange that they brought us straight here. We didn't even go to the police station. We weren't formally arrested, nothing like that."

Allissa agreed, slumping into the seat. Her eyes rested on a large screen on the wall in front of them. A couple in silhouette walked hand in hand along a beach at sunset.

"We've got involved in something that's way above our heads here." Leo slouched down beside Allissa. "The police, conspiracy theories — we just find missing people." His fingers tapped an erratic pattern on his knees. "How long until our —"

"We solve mysteries," Allissa interrupted. "And sometimes those mysteries involve governments, the police, whoever. There's still a mystery here."

"Where is Fasslane?"

"Who helped him disappear and why?" Allissa interrupted.

The image of the beach on the big screen faded, and a news report appeared. A few short words summarized the world's headlines. Protests and riots continued on a global scale as the information in Fasslane's book found its way around the world.

"This is going to be trouble," Allissa said, pointing at the screen.

"But what can we —" The words dried up in Leo's mouth.

"I don't know, yet." Allissa tapped her lips. "Something will come up."

The news report faded to black. The screen remained empty for several seconds and then a cursor flashed in the top left-hand corner. Leo watched it, his sense of worry burgeoning. He glanced sideways at Allissa. She also watched the cursor on the screen.

Then, letter by letter, simple white text emerged. It appeared as though someone was typing it live into the system.

You are in danger.

The words came slowly, then for a few moments the cursor stood still, blinking.

Leo's breath caught in his throat. His eyes remained riveted to the screen. Colour drained from his face. His hands, which moments ago danced in frustration, lay dead still in his lap. He tried to swallow, but a lump of concrete had formed in his throat.

Another phrase appeared on the screen.

Those men were not police.

The cursor paused again.

Look in your bags.

The cursor blinked twice, and then the video of the beach returned to the screen. Leo and Allissa looked at each other, eyebrows raised, eyes wide.

"What was —" Leo's voice trailed off. He eyed the bag on the seat beside him.

Allissa was the first to move. She grabbed her bag from the seat next to her and tore it open. A few items of clothing, carelessly stuffed on top, fell to the floor. She pushed her hand deeper into the bag. Her expression paled further.

"There's something here," she whispered. "It's cold, and... sort of solid. Like a brick. It's pretty heavy too."

Allissa yanked out more of the carelessly packed clothes. She pushed her hands in again and pulled the foreign item to the top.

In the cold light of the departure lounge she recognised the white, plastic covered, brick-shaped object from gangster films. Drugs...

Allissa fumbled with the object, stuffing it back inside the bag. She glanced around the lounge and then looked at Leo. Her jaw hung limp.

Leo tried to speak. His mouth made the shape of the words, but no sound came forth. He struggled to breathe. It felt as though the air had been removed from the room. The noise of the airport shrunk to a distant murmur.

"Look," Allissa said, pointing back at the screen. The video faded, and the text appeared again.

Leo. the writing came at the same speed as before. *Right trouser pocket.*

For a long moment, as though the events were happening to someone else and not him, Leo stared unmoving at the screen.

The text faded to black, and the news report occupied the screen again.

"Quickly, look," Allissa snapped, shaking his arm.

Leo shook himself back into focus. He dug his fingers into his pocket as the video had instructed. His hand closed around something unfamiliar. The object was hard and about the same size and shape as an egg. Leo pulled it out, holding it low to keep it out of sight.

It was made of hard, white plastic. Leo ran a finger across it and flicked up the top. It sprung open, revealing a pair of cordless earbuds.

Leo fished one out and wedged it in his ear. Allissa took the other.

"About time. Listen closely now." The man's familiar voice came through the earbuds as clear as day. "If we've got any chance of getting you out of there, you must do exactly as I say."

43

Burak pounded his fist against the steering wheel as they waited at the airport security checkpoint. Beyond the chain-link fence, vehicles rumbled back towards the city. An airport security guard approached the driver's window. Burak rolled down the glass.

"Can I see your ID please, officer?" said the guard, an automatic rifle strapped to his chest.

Burak slid a hand inside his jacket pocket and produced the ID card. He was confident there would be no problem. It was an expensive forgery, with the electronic record to go with it.

"Thank you, officer," the guard said, taking a cursory look at the card. The guard raised a hand to his colleague behind the blackened glass of the office. The gate rumbled open.

Burak nodded, stashed his ID back in his pocket, and pulled the truck through the gate and out in the direction of the city.

Watching the airport grow small in the mirror, Burak thought about the two detectives. They would be sitting now, bewildered and possibly scared, in the departure lounge, waiting for their flight. They wouldn't even see what was coming for them.

Burak pulled his phone from the pocket of his jacket and dialled a number from memory. He held the phone against his ear as it rung three times.

"What?" came a gruff male voice.

"They are in position. Make the call. Do exactly what I told you. Do not deviate from the plan, okay?"

Heavy breathing strained down the line.

"I am not an idiot, I understand. I do this and we are even. You do not call me again."

The line went dead.

Burak snapped the indicator, pulled the truck onto the motorway, and then placed another call.

"Is it done?" Esin's urgent voice piped through the line. Burak imagined her sitting in the office, waiting for his call.

"Yes, it is done," Burak grunted, raising his voice against the rumbling truck. "The police will be with them in a few minutes. They will not be bothering us again."

"Excellent," Esin said. "Get back here as soon as possible. We are moving tonight."

44

"I know you'll have a lot of questions." The man's voice was clear and crisp, as though coming from the next room. "I promise you that soon you'll get to ask them all. Right now, though, we're in a bit of a difficult situation. Did you check your bags?"

"Yes," Allissa said. "How did you know?"

"It's an old trick they've pulled many times. If they can't get what they want from you, they'll get *you* for something. Plus, it discredits you. People don't tend to believe the opinions of drug smugglers. I expect there will be something in the region of five kilograms in both your bags. By the time you get out of prison in, say, twenty years, this will all be a distant memory."

Leo paled further. His hands gripped the armrests.

"We're listening," Allissa said. "What do we do?"

"First, we need to get you out of there." The clack of typing keys came down the line.

"Not this again," Leo said. "No jumping between buildings this time."

"I'll do my best, but a team of the real police are already

on their way."

"How do you know all of this?" Allissa asked.

"I have access to the airport's security cameras. I don't have time to explain properly now. Soon, though. Okay, remove any tags and shove your bags beneath the seats. Taking them with you will only slow you down."

Leo and Allissa nodded at each other and did as they were instructed.

"Okay, behind you, boarding for a flight to Amsterdam has almost completed. Gate 14. Without drawing unnecessary attention to yourself, get up and walk towards the gate. Look casual."

Leo and Allissa complied. Allissa looked around the departure lounge. A few passengers milled around gate 14, but most had already boarded. Through the window, the colourful tail of the aircraft shone in the early evening light. For a moment Allissa wished they had the sort of simple life which allowed weekend trips to cities like Amsterdam.

"Good, get just a little closer," the man said. Leo and Allissa were twenty feet from the gate now. The attendant, checking boarding passes and passports, hadn't even looked their way.

Another sound flooded the quiet of the departure lounge. Instantly, both Allissa and Leo knew what it was. The sound of running feet. They turned to face the sound. For a few seconds, nothing changed, then several policemen charged into the lounge.

"We need to get out of here," strained Allissa's voice.

"Yep, give me a few seconds. I'm monitoring their communications frequency. They haven't seen you yet. This should do it..."

A high-pitched squeal jarred through the terminal. It oscillated between two piercing tones. Allissa looked around. The other passengers glanced about frantically. Some shuffled towards emergency exits, others waited for instructions. The attendant at gate 14 snatched up a handset and shouted into it.

"Go now, through the gate. Now."

Allissa charged at the door. Leo followed closely on her tail. The airport attendant, now facing the other way, didn't even notice.

Leo and Allissa barged through the door and ran for a ramp directly ahead of them. The door clanged closed behind them, muffling the chaotic noise of the departure lounge.

Allissa glanced over her shoulder; Leo ran two steps behind her. No one else had made it through the door yet. They turned right into the umbilical corridor that connected the plane to the airport. Footsteps thundered on the metal walkway.

"There's a door on your left, now," said the voice. "Then down the stairs."

Allissa and Leo pushed through the door and onto a metal staircase. Allissa glanced around them. The staircase ran down the side of the building to the concrete below. Behind them, the giant aircraft sat ready to depart. The whine of jet engines filled the air. Several members of airport staff wearing high-vis jackets stood just feet away.

"Go now," the voice demanded. Allissa ran down the stairs, her feet clanging against the metal. Leo followed. Reaching the bottom, they slipped out of sight behind a concrete pillar.

Allissa listened closely, expecting to hear the crack of the door above them and the thump of their pursuers' boots on the stairs. Her pulse pounded in her ears. So far, the sound hadn't come.

"Good, just stay there for a moment. I don't think they've seen you."

Allissa glanced around the pillar. To their right, the aircraft crew completed the final pre-take off tasks. To their left, a roadway for service vehicles ran between the terminal building and the aeroplane. The thud of a diesel engine approached from the roadway. Allissa pushed her back into the pillar, her hands flat against the cool concrete.

"There's a truck coming," the voice said. "It's going to stop next to you. The back door's unlocked. Get in."

Allissa and Leo looked at each other, both thinking the same. They'd just been bundled from one truck and into the airport. Climbing into another to get away made them uneasy at best.

A truck wheezed and spluttered to a stop beside them. *Alpha Airport Services* was just visible beneath a layer of dust.

Allissa peered around the pillar again. All the airport staff were engaged in their tasks. She glanced from the truck to the aeroplane again, pulled a deep breath to steel herself, then ran around to the rear of the vehicle. She leapt behind the vehicle and out of sight, then pulled open the door. As the voice had told them, it was unlocked. Allissa scrambled inside and Leo followed. Allissa glanced around the truck's interior. Boxes and crates lay against the walls. Leo shut the door, and the light inside the truck sunk to a dull gloom. The engine growled, and the truck rolled forwards. The crates rattled and slid with the motion. Allissa reached out for one of the walls to steady herself.

"A friend of yours?" Allissa asked as the truck gained speed.

"Someone loyal to our cause," replied the voice. "Get comfortable. She will drop you where you need to go."

45

Esin stood from her desk and walked across to the window. The city through the glass dimmed with the dying day. Lights on the streets and boulevards below shimmered in neon swathes. Esin looked out towards the Bosphorus and the shores of Asia beyond. That's where they'd be heading in a couple of hours. From there the plan was simple; head out to her mountain cabin in Uludağ, where a fresh car and enough supplies for several weeks had already been prepared. Then what Fasslane did was up to him. Esin would be pleased to see the back of him, to leave him to his own devices. Since he'd been hauled up here, all he'd done was moan.

After a short stay in Uludağ, he would head overland and into the anonymous chaos of Asia, Esin imagined. Once there, he could be anyone he wanted, as long as he stopped being Brent Fasslane. The payments Esin had agreed to deposit in a private bank account each month would make that worth his while and reduce the temptation to go back to his old ways. It was just a small percentage of what Sadik-

Tech stood to make when fear and unrest reached boiling point, and the government needed help sorting it out.

Fasslane was a loose end, though, Esin thought, studying her flawlessly painted fingernails. For now, he was a necessary one, but not for long. Loose ends had two options: they either got tucked in and didn't cause any further problems, or they got snipped off.

Esin dug her red fingernails into the flesh of her thumb. She would give Fasslane the opportunity to tuck himself in quietly — he may be useful again in the future — or she would waste no time snipping him off.

The smartphone trilled from the desk behind her. Esin turned and glanced at it, glowing in the gloom. A fission of worry passed through her body. Despite the warm office, she shivered.

She strode back over to the desk and snagged up the phone. The call was from one of her police informants. She answered and held the phone to her ear.

"They've gone," came a breathless male voice down the line.

Esin balled her fists, digging her fingernails deep into her hands. "What do you mean, they've gone?"

"I don't have time to explain." Another voice shouted in the background. The voices became muffled. A few seconds later, the informant returned to the call. "I don't know how, but they've disappeared."

"What do you mean they've disappeared?" Esin barked. Her nails dug harder into the flesh of her palm.

The line was silent for a moment. An alarm shrieked in the background and people shouted.

"I don't know. I have to go. I'll tell you when I know more." The line went dead.

Esin's lips curled into a snarl. She threw the phone

across the office. The sound of smashing glass filled the room.

"Burak, why haven't you sorted this?" Esin hissed again, her nails cut into her palm. Sharp pain jarred from her hands.

She glanced across the office. The phone had collided with the picture of Ahmet Sadik in the community centre. Both now lay amid shards of glass on the floor. Esin snatched up the phone and examined it. It was largely unscathed. She unlocked the screen and scrolled to Burak's number. A drop of blood smeared across the screen.

Esin paused and turned her hand over. Blood pooled in her palm from a small gash. Then the photograph on the floor caught Esin's eye. Sadik smiled up from beneath the shards of glass. He was mocking her from beyond the grave.

46

THE TRUCK RUMBLED forwards for several minutes and then slowed. Eventually, with the hissing of brakes, it stopped completely.

"Security checkpoint," came the voice in the headphones. "Stay quiet."

A male voice, speaking Turkish, reverberated through the truck's narrow body. A female voice answered. The man and the woman exchanged several words.

"They want to look in the back," the voice in the headphones hissed urgently. "Get out of sight."

Leo glanced around. There was no light inside the truck. Translucent panels in the roof provided the only light. Leo examined the racks and boxes, haphazardly strewn throughout the truck.

Leo noticed a large pile of boxes towards the front of the truck. He signalled to Allissa and they both silently made their way forwards. The boxes may provide a hiding space for a cursory look. If the truck was searched thoroughly, they would be found in less than a minute.

Outside the truck, footsteps thumped from the cab to

the rear door. The male voice shouted again, more violently this time.

Leo turned to face the noise and missed a step, sending a pair of crates tumbling to the floor. The crash echoed, deep and sonorous, through the chassis. The footsteps stopped and a deep silence followed.

Leo and Allissa looked at each other, all colour draining from their expressions.

"I wish I knew what they were saying," Allissa whispered under her breath.

One of the guards shouted again. Finally, the driver's door clicked and a pair of softer footsteps dropped to the concrete.

Leo placed the next few steps with incredible care. He and Allissa crawled in behind the stack of boxes.

The lighter footsteps had reached the rear of the truck. Keys jangled.

Leo remembered how they'd got straight into the truck. The search for keys was clearly buying Leo and Allissa time to hide.

Allissa pulled her arms and legs in tight. Leo did the same.

A key crunched in the lock and the locking mechanism clicked. The truck's rear door swung open. The thick beam of a powerful torch shone into the darkness.

Leo held his breath. He heard Allissa do the same.

A footstep clanged through the chassis. The truck swayed backwards. The footsteps thudded inside the truck. The torch beam swung this way and that. A box fell and skittered across the floor. The hefty boots continued moving.

The female voice protested.

The torch swept across the stacked crates again and

rested on the wall behind Leo and Allissa. Another footstep thudded through the truck. A box crashed to the floor, its contents bouncing around the truck bed.

Leo's lungs ached, begging him to breathe.

The man took another step closer. Leo could hear the man's breathing now. It was deep and rasping in the silent truck. The pile of crates concealing Leo and Allissa started to move. The man picked up a box and threw it across the truck. It crashed against the far wall.

The female voice protested more aggressively now.

Leo listened closely to the man's heavy breathing. Another box crashed to the floor.

A radio squawked and then a distant, tinny voice filled the truck. The man stopped searching and stood. The torch beam came to rest on the floor beside Leo.

The man snapped the radio from his belt and barked his reply. A tinny voice answered.

The man grumbled something unintelligible, and the footsteps thundered their way back towards the door.

The truck's rear doors slammed closed.

Leo let his breath go and inhaled greedily. He still didn't risk moving. Allissa's head lay in her hands.

Short footsteps padded back around the truck and climbed into the cab.

A fist banged twice on the side of the vehicle. The engine whined, and they pulled away.

"We're clear," said the voice in his headphones. "That was closer than I'd expected it to be. This must have really rattled them."

Leo took another two deep breaths and sat up against the wall of the truck. Allissa sat beside him. For several minutes, neither spoke.

The vehicle swayed onwards, jarring Leo's spine with

each bump of the road. Leo glanced at Allissa, sitting beside him, and for the second time today tried to work out where they were going. Back to the city, he assumed, although nothing today was turning out how he might expect.

Eventually, the truck banged and wheezed to a stop. The handbrake crunched, and the engine coughed into silence. The driver's door screeched open, and someone jumped to the ground. The locking mechanism of the rear door clicked, and the door swung open. Then light footsteps padded away.

Leo and Allissa looked at each other. Leo climbed shakily to his feet, his muscles aching from the uncomfortable journey, and his nerves still sensitive from the stress of the day. He reached the door and scrambled down to the concrete. He turned, extending a hand to Allissa.

They were in a backstreet. Lights shone from the windows above them. In the distance, a mosque's minaret pierced the skyline. Something scuttled in the darkness. A strong, cool breeze drifted past. Leo inhaled the distant scent of the sea.

"Where are we?" he asked.

"Sultanahmet, Istanbul," the voice in the headset replied.

"Back where we started," Allissa added. "Why are we here?"

"The answers are coming very soon. Walk to your right. There's a blue door."

Leo and Allissa turned and squinted into the darkness. Metal shutters, no doubt loading bays for shops or restaurants, lined the narrow street. Large bins overflowed with rubbish. Something scurried beneath one of the bins. The sickly smell of rotting waste hung in the air.

Jarring, painful memories shot into Leo's mind. This

street felt horribly similar to one they'd visited in Kathmandu some years before. That visit hadn't ended well. Leo forced the thought from his mind and stared off into the darkness.

Somewhere in the shadows a door clicked and swung open. A rectangle of light appeared. A small figure stood silhouetted in the light.

"Over here," came the calm voice, now carrying through the still evening air. "Good to meet you. My name is Ramiz, and as promised, it's time I gave you some answers."

47

"Come in, come in. I am sorry for all this cloak and dagger stuff. I was hoping meeting you wouldn't be quite this difficult."

Leo and Allissa stepped into the bright light of a shop's back room. Ramiz, the man they had only known from his voice, was small, with quick features, and a head that seemed slightly too big for his body.

"Follow me," Ramiz said, leading them into the shop. Ornate rugs and textiles of various colours and designs covered every surface. Ramiz led them to the far end of the shop. A thick drape in red and gold covered the wall. Ramiz pulled the fabric aside and stepped behind it. Leo and Allissa followed.

The room was a textile workshop. Needles and threads covered a large table in the centre. Tools hung on the walls.

"You make these fabrics here?" Leo asked.

"The man who owns this shop repairs them. He is an old friend of my father's, so when I was looking for a place to... you'll see... he suggested this."

Allissa picked up a stretch of red and gold embroidered fabric.

"There's a lucrative trade in antique textiles. The repairs can often be long and arduous, but they're worth it to see something like this enjoy a second life." Ramiz pointed at a small rug, depicting an elephant with a man on its back, which lay on the table in a state of mid-completion. "But that's not what we're here to discuss." Ramiz leaned against the table and pushed. Despite his meagre size, the table slid easily across the floor.

Leo and Allissa stepped to the edge of the room and watched. Beneath the table, in the floor of the workshop, a hole emerged.

"I wasn't expecting that," Leo said, gazing down at a staircase, neatly cut into the floor of the workshop. Lights illuminated the tunnel, as though it were an exhibition in a museum.

"That's the beauty of it," Ramiz said, a smile lighting his face. "In the 1960s, my father's friend bought this land and set about building the new premises."

They stepped down into the staircase. Ramiz's voice echoed fitfully around the roughly cut space. After a dozen or so steps, Leo glanced up at the workshop behind them. They were already at least a storey underground. The passage continued for some time yet. Cool air drifted up to meet them.

Leo focused on his footing on the uneven staircase. Sweat beads sprouted on his brow.

Ramiz reached the bottom of the staircase and paused before a door. Leo snuck a glance over his shoulder. The workshop had been reduced to a small circle of light. He couldn't estimate the distance they've travelled, but knew it was several storeys at least.

"During the work they discovered this —" Ramiz drew back a bolt on the thick steel door. A deep clang rumbled around the cave. Ramiz pushed open the door, the hinges squealing, and stepped inside.

Leo and Allissa followed. Surprise stopped them in their tracks.

"Wow," Leo whispered, his voice sibilant. His eyes scanned the space, trying to make sense of it.

The roof, supported by pillars flanking both sides, arched somewhere overhead. The walls were constructed of large stones, chipped meticulously by hand. Giant slabs covered the floor. Leo took a step forward and pulled a deep breath of damp, cool air.

"It's a cistern dating back to the Byzantine era," Ramiz said. "It was used, alongside many others, to hold water, should the city ever fall under siege. People were very inventive back then. This is one of the smaller ones. We think it was probably built for a particular household who once owned this site."

"This place is amazing," Allissa stated, crossing to one of the walls. She ran her hand across the stone and then rubbed her dry fingers. "And no one knows about it?"

"That's right, my father's friend considered opening it to public display, but seeing how many of the city's old buildings had been ruined by tourism, he decided to keep it quiet. He didn't want all sorts of people traipsing down here. I think he liked the idea that it was our little bit of old Byzantium."

"It used to be filled with water?" Leo asked.

"Yes, it was full when it was discovered. The draining tunnel, which leads down to the Golden Horn, was cleared out, and the inlet pipes have been sealed." Ramiz pointed at a row of metal plates high on the back wall. "There's an underground river sealed behind there."

"What do these mean?" Allissa pointed to a carving on the far wall. The indentations were worn into illegibility, but clearly made by hand.

"There are several stones in here with ornate carvings. These places were often made with recycled stone brought here from one of the conquered lands. That could have been part of a temple a few hundred miles away. We don't know where for sure."

"Fascinating stuff," Allissa said, nodding and wide-eyed.

"But" — Ramiz clapped his hands; the sound rang harsh in the enclosed space — "I didn't bring you to talk about fallen civilisations, but to discuss with you how we can stop our society from sharing the same fate. This way, please." Ramiz led Leo and Allissa to the far end of the giant cistern where, as yet unnoticed, several desks contained computer equipment. Ramiz tapped a keyboard and multiple monitors sprung into life.

"Now that's a cool set up," Leo said, examining Ramiz's four displays mounted on extendable arms.

"Wait a second," Allissa said, her arms folded. "Okay, so I admit I was a little distracted for a moment there by this amazing place, but we need some answers from you. This time yesterday we were drinking beers in Galata. Now, we've been kidnapped twice and are pretty much international fugitives."

"You're quite right," Ramiz said. "Let me explain."

48

"We're here and will soon have the information we need," Burak barked into the phone.

Esin grumbled a reply and the line went dead.

She was angry, and for good reason. The bumbling detectives had gotten away — that was not acceptable. Their presence threatened the plan. Burak fumed. He had done everything right. It had all gone perfectly to plan. The detectives had been deposited at the airport, with enough contraband to do a decent spell inside. They should be languishing in a cell now, not rampaging through the city, intent on ruining things.

Burak snarled, tensed his arms, and strode through the office of the Istanbul Transport Authority. He approached a bank of screens, each showing a different part of the city. One of his men held the technician by the back of his shirt. Blood dribbled from the man's mouth and into his thin beard. The poor guy had chosen to work the wrong shift tonight.

Burak nodded and the other man let the technician go. The young technician sprawled to the floor. Burak snatched him up, lifting him by the throat, and shoved him against the wall.

"You will help us, and maybe you'll live." Burak's hands closed around the small man's neck.

The technician nodded uselessly.

"Once I have my information, we will be out of here. But... if you do anything to get in my way, you and your friends will be found floating in the Bosphorus." Burak nodded at the other technician and the two-man security team. The three men stared back from the corner of the room, their glassy eyes widening with fear.

Burak and his thugs had stormed the office a few minutes ago and quickly bound and gagged them all. Hidden in the basement of a government building in Menderes, Istanbul's transport monitoring station was quiet at this time of night.

One of the security men groaned from behind his gag. Burak's thug stepped over and kicked the man hard in the stomach. The man slumped to the floor, wheezing.

"We'll be out of here in ten minutes with your co-operation," Burak said, examining the technician. "Do you understand?"

The man nodded, whimpering.

Burak dropped the man into a chair in front of the glowing screens.

"I need to trace a vehicle which left the airport this evening." Burak looked over the man's shoulder at the screens. The flickering images showed different parts of the city. Burak glanced at the control console.

"That could be thousands," the technician muttered, his hands tapping at the keyboard.

"I expect they'll have come from the restricted side,"

Burak said, also giving the technician a time period to search.

The technician nodded. Cameras from around the airport filled the screen.

"Two vehicles left through the airside entrance during that time. A police vehicle, and some kind of service truck." The technician pointed at the screen. "Alpha Airport Services, it says on the side."

Burak's hand crashed against the desk. He leaned in and examined the vehicle. "I need to know where this truck goes. Can you do that?"

Just fifteen minutes later, Burak and his men pushed through the building's rear door and towards their waiting car.

49

"I am in a very fortunate position. Some years ago, I inherited a sum of money that allows me to follow certain passions."

Allissa nodded in a way that said, *get on with it.*

"In recent years Turkey has seen an unprecedented rise in corruption. I don't necessarily mean corruption in terms of money, I mean the corruption of truth. Sure, everywhere in the modern world lies are told in the media. But here in Turkey they are told blatantly, without any real attempt to cover them up. And our people, we are so used to it, so bored by it, that we just shrug and carry on.

"Five years ago, after an attempted coup tried to overthrow our president, largely based on lies and misinformation, I decided that I had to do something about it. So, I set up my small group — The Guardians of Truth." Ramiz pointed at the largest screen in the centre of his desk. A logo rotated slowly.

"We now have a small team of journalists here and across the country who check whether the claims people make are true. We post the results — the truth as we have been, honestly and impartially, able to understand it — on our website and social media platforms. Clearly, this has not made me very popular with certain people. Fortunately, to this day, using VPN technology and other digital rerouting, I've been able to remain anonymous."

"Okay, that's one thing," Allissa said. "But drones and hacking into the airport's security?"

"Yes, this is the biggest operation we have ever had to do. When I heard that Brent Fasslane was to speak in Istanbul, I knew there would be trouble. As you may know, relations between Turkey and the United States have soured in the last few years. Our leader does not like theirs, or something like that," — Ramiz shrugged — "but this man..." He tapped a key and a picture of Brent Fasslane appeared on the screen. "The egotistical maniac that he is, had managed to worm his way into the middle of it."

"The Americans wanted him back, but the Turkish government said no, right?"

"That's correct," Ramiz said. "There was some nonsense about a trade with a man of Turkish origin, but I think it's probably just a play of power. After a lot of nonsense, all both sides had managed to do was provide a man, one with a real score to settle, the biggest audience on the planet. Everyone was watching him."

"And then he went missing," Leo said.

"Exactly. The Turkish blame the Americans, the Americans deny it all, no one knows who to believe, so they turn to the blatant lies told by an angry little man." Ramiz pointed at the screen again.

"Can one man really make that much difference, on a global scale?" Allissa asked. "Sure, this is embarrassing, but could it cause —"

"War?" Ramiz interrupted. "War is not caused by a

single event. It's fuelled by a growing mistrust, lack of communication, and then something pushes it over the edge. This may not cause all-out war right now, but believe me, if we don't stop this man and whoever else is behind him, it will come. This is just the beginning. The wedge which he is driving between Turkey and America will force Turkey over to the great Asian powers."

"China," Leo said.

"We will again see a world divided in two. This is the biggest threat our society has faced in the last sixty years."

"Okay, okay," Allissa said, her palms out. "Let's not get ahead of ourselves here. He's just one bloke. A loudmouth idiot."

Ramiz nodded. "Who has already forced politicians from their positions, caused stock market crashes, and sent people rioting in the streets. He needs to be stopped."

"But how?" Leo said.

"We have to prove he's alive. We have to prove that his disappearance was all a front. All smoke and mirrors, as they say."

50

BURAK CLIMBED out of the car and peered down the unlit backstreet. Discoloured metal shutters covered the loading bays of several shops. A bedraggled cat scurried through the shadows, sending a used tin can clanging across the concrete.

The other men scrambled out of the car too.

Burak turned and looked up at the camera on the wall of the opposite building. The thing was pointing in the opposite direction, but the footage showed the truck arriving here from the airport, and then leaving a few minutes later.

Burak pulled a torch from his pocket and clicked it on. He swept the beam across the street until he saw what he was looking for, thick tyre tracks on the filth-covered concrete.

"They were here," Burak hissed, swinging his torch down the backstreet. "We're close, I can tell. Follow me."

51

"I'm with you," Leo said. Allissa and Ramiz turned to face him. "I totally think we should out this dude as the troublemaker he is, but how?"

Ramiz extended a finger and pointed at Leo. "Ahh, well, that's where I can help you. Take a seat." He indicated two chairs beside his own.

Leo and Allissa sat down. Ramiz tapped at the keyboard for a few seconds and a video filled the screen.

"Drone footage," Allissa said, watching dark streets of Istanbul move beneath the camera.

"Yes, from the night Fasslane disappeared."

The drone slowed and then hovered over the building. Allissa didn't recognise the building from the air.

"That's the Hagia Sophia." Ramiz pointed at the screen. "Each of these drones only has around thirty minutes battery life, so we work them in rotation, like shifts. This is the third one. Okay, watch now. You'll see Fasslane leaving."

Ramiz enlarged the image on the screen. Sure enough, a moment later Fasslane and his guards shuffled out of back door and around to the vehicles.

"Yes, we saw this from the security camera. He gets in one side of the vehicle and then straight out of the other."

"Yes," Ramiz said, shooting Leo a glance, "but did you see what happened next?"

Leo shook his head.

"They climb through the vehicle, as you said. It's a classic trick. And then watch this." Ramiz tapped the keyboard to increase the brightness of the footage. Fasslane and his two security men ran to the back of the final armoured vehicle, and then scurried in the direction of the gate. The drone followed them.

"There's the explosion," Ramiz said, pointing out a flare on the screen. The drone wobbled for a few seconds before steading itself again. "Fortunately, the drone had already moved away from the vehicles by that point. There's Fasslane, look."

He pointed at three figures, crouching in the shadows at the rear of the building.

"Wait for it, look at this."

A truck screeched to a stop on the outside of the fence. The back door swung open. Fasslane and his two guards darted from the shadows and into the vehicle.

"Hold on, pause that," Allissa shouted, squinting at the screen.

Ramiz hit the space bar and the image froze.

"Can you back it up just a little?"

Ramiz prodded at the keyboard and the image juddered backwards.

"Zoom in on that guy."

The image of the leading guard filled the screen. His face was set into a snarl of concentration, his jaw jutting forwards. Ramiz changed some settings and the picture lightened.

"See the scar," Allissa said, pointing at the screen.

"It's the police officer!" Leo stated. "The so-called police officer who dragged us from the Grand Bazaar today. Do you know where they went?"

"Of course." Ramiz hit play and steepled his fingers. "The police truck cut through the traffic away from the Hagia Sophia. Two emergency vehicles squealed past them in the other direction, lights strobing."

"If you know all of this, why can't you just reveal it yourself?" Allissa asked.

Ramiz paused the footage. "And lose the gift of my anonymity? No, I need to stay undercover. I need this to get out without anyone knowing where it came from."

"Couldn't you just give it to one of the newspapers?" Leo asked.

"This is too important. I need someone I can trust to deliver it to the right people and keep making noise until it's taken seriously."

Leo leaned back in the chair and thought about Marcus Green. He was just the right person to reveal this to the world. "I think we can help you with that. So, where does this guy end up?"

The truck on the screen turned onto a dual carriage way. They accelerated into the evening's light traffic.

"Now, that's where this gets very interesting," Ramiz said, leaning backwards.

At that moment, a slow clap reverberated around the cistern. It was soon followed by a deep peel of laughter.

"This is where you've been hiding, yeah. Underground, like the rats that you are."

52

Leo's heart leapt into his throat. He would recognise that voice anywhere. He turned slowly in his chair.

"You set us up," Allissa snarled. "We'd be in prison now if you'd got your way."

Burak tilted his head back and laughed again, his face crinkled by the scar. The man had changed out of the police uniform and now wore a loose-fitting shirt, jacket, and trousers. Two men stood behind him, cradling semi-automatic weapons.

"That, I think is, the problem with our system, isn't it? You put on a uniform, and suddenly everyone trusts you. It is all too easy! What someone wears is no way to tell what's in here." He tapped his chest with thick knuckles.

Ramiz sat quietly in his chair, his back to Burak and his men.

"But this has worked out better than I would ever have imagined." Burak focused on Ramiz. "If my assumptions are correct, you are the esteemed Guardians of Truth. You have been a frustration to my employer for some time. This is your secret headquarters, yeah?"

Ramiz turned around in his chair.

Watching closely, Allissa noticed Burak paused for a second. His eyes focused in on Ramiz, as though not quite believing what he saw. Then, his mouth twisted into something of a smile. He examined the stonework of the ancient cistern. "I like it, it's very..." — his hand drew circles in the air as though searching physically for the word — "It's very fitting."

Ramiz, who had sat quietly since the intrusion, suddenly exploded with energy. He spun around and started typing feverously. Images flashed across the screen. A loading bar appeared beneath the image of a padlock.

"Stop what you're doing now," Burak screamed, pulling a gun from his hip.

"No way, you're not getting this information. We will take you down with this."

The loading bar on the screen crept from right to left.

Burak pointed his gun in the air and squeezed off several shots. The gun roared and fragments of rock skittered to the floor. "Stop it now, or I will shoot you," Burak shouted.

Ramiz tapped the keyboard several more times. The screens faded to black. He spun around on his chair and stood up, arms folded.

"Done," he said.

"Look at that," Leo said, pointing at the wall on the far side of the cistern. Two bullets had punctured the metal covering the cistern's old inlet. Water poured through the holes. As Leo watched, the metal covering cracked, and the stream of the water became a torrent.

"Take these computers, quickly." Burak snarled at his men. One of them rushed across, his weapon dropping to his side, and unplugged the computer's processing unit.

"We have some of the world's best hackers; they'll get through this in no time," Burak shouted.

It was Ramiz's turn to laugh now. "Let them try," he said, staring hard at Burak. "By the time you crack this, they will have shared this information with the world." He pointed at Leo and Allissa.

A twisted smile crept onto Burak's face. "I don't think so." He pulled a smartphone from his pocket. "You see that? No signal."

"Wait, what?" Ramiz shrugged.

"From down here, they won't be able to do anything." Burak shouted instructions at his men. They raised their guns and stepped backwards towards the door. "And just to make sure you don't cause any more trouble, you're coming with me." Burak seized Ramiz by the arm. The smaller man yelped and stumbled like a rag doll. Burak dragged him towards the door.

Burak reached the door and turned back to Leo and Allissa.

Water covered the floor now, its surface glinting darkly.

Burak's mouth distorted into an ugly grin, the scar disfiguring the left side of it.

Allissa glanced around the room. The old cistern, true to its purpose, was filling quickly. She stepped forward. Water lapped around her ankles, cold and menacing against her skin.

"You're really going to wish you hadn't come to Istanbul," Burak said, shuffling backwards toward the staircase.

Allissa looked from the impenetrable steel door to Leo. She nodded almost imperceptibly. At the gesture, the pair charged forward, feet sloshing through the water. Guns howled. Burak and his men fired into the cistern, bullets thudding into the stone.

Leo and Allissa froze, their ears ringing from the deafening explosions.

As the reverberations died out, Burak grinned wider than ever. Then he slammed the door.

53

THE SOUND of the slamming door reverberated noisily around the ancient walls of the cistern. The crunch of the door's locking mechanism followed. Then footsteps retreated somewhere beyond, joined by the faint whimpering of Ramiz being dragged up the stairs.

Allissa rushed up to the door and inspected the steel. There was no handle, lock or even a keyhole on the inside. The steel was smooth and modern, obviously fitted when the cistern was rediscovered just a few decades ago.

Allissa ran her fingers around the door's edge, looking for a weak spot or something she could grab on to. There was nothing. It was well fitted and strong.

The sound of footsteps on the stairs faded into nothing. The torrents of water murmured from the stone. Something behind them cracked, boomed and splashed.

Leo and Allissa spun around to see another great chunk of rock fall away from the bullet-riddled walls. The water gushed through with greater ferocity now. It bubbled and churned, rising with each moment.

Leo and Allissa looked at each other.

Leo's Adam's apple bobbed, as though he was trying to swallow but couldn't.

Allissa knew the feeling. A dull fear gripped her stomach. Sure, they'd escaped several potentially lethal situations, but being trapped then drowned in an ancient cistern no one knew existed? That didn't sound appealing.

"We need to make a full inspection of this place," Allissa shouted over the sound of the water, which had now turned from a murmur into a roar. She raised her voice against the onset of fear. "Ramiz said those stairs were carved out in the 1960s, right?"

Leo nodded, his face ashen, the muscles in his shoulders standing rigid.

"There must have been a way to get in here before that." Allissa looked up at the ceiling, looming far above them. "If this existed all that time without being discovered, I bet the entrance tunnel did too." Allissa instructed Leo to start his search on the opposite side of the cistern. "Look for anything unusual. A different type of rock, or something that looks as though it's been covered up."

Allissa sloshed through the water. It was almost up to her knees now and made moving about difficult. It was cold too. A shudder clawed its way up her spine.

Leo moved to the cistern's far wall and ran his hands across the roughly hewn stone. The cistern was constructed in large blocks of mismatched colours and sizes. Each would be too big for a single person, or even a pair of people to move on their own. He glanced up at the ceiling, arching overhead. He took a deep breath in an attempt to quell his rising anxiety. His chest felt as though tons of rock and rubble were pressing down on top of him.

He counted to three and tried again, pulling the damp smelling air in through his nose and out through his mouth.

The influx of oxygen helped. He returned to his search, examining the walls as closely as he could. It didn't help that the cistern was lit only by a few spotlights in the centre. Most of the walls lay in gloom.

Leo moved along the first section of wall quickly. The stones were solid. No modern mortar indicated they blocked any tunnel or passage. Nothing.

He lumbered across to the next section of wall, sending great splashes around the space. The water lapped above his knees now. Each step dragged him further and further down, as though the water was pulling him into an embrace.

He repeated the process, examining each stone in turn.

"You see anything?" Allissa asked, her voice strained against the thunderous torrent.

"Nothing," Leo said, peering at her over his shoulder. They were moving around the room in opposite directions and would meet somewhere on the far wall, opposite the door. They had searched over half the cistern now. With a growing sense of helplessness, Leo questioned how visible any old access routes would be after countless centuries.

Across the room, Allissa pushed on. The water lapped over her waist now. Her teeth chattered and she struggled to keep her hands from shaking. The pleasant warm air of autumnal Istanbul didn't penetrate this far below ground. Preserved from the ravages of weather by the ground above, most of the stones were as solid as they had been centuries ago. Maybe this was it? Maybe this was the case that pushed them over the edge. Surely, there were only so many times you could dodge a bullet and come out unscathed?

Allissa glanced over at Leo. Unshed tears tugged at the corners of her eyes.

Maybe they should have just gotten out while they had

the chance. This job had brought them together; maybe now it was time to do something normal, something safe.

Her thoughts were interrupted by a voice. Leo's voice, strained against the hammering water. Allissa muted a sob and met Leo's eyes. Her face contorted in hope as he said,

"I think I've found something."

54

Allissa charged across the cistern, turning the water milky white. Rising above her hips, it made movement difficult. Soon it would be quicker to swim. She reached Leo and put her hand on his shoulder. His skin beneath the t-shirt was warm. Heat flowed through Allissa's body, dissipating her negative thoughts. They would do this. They had to do this.

"There, look, I think it's something," Leo said, pointing upwards.

Allissa squinted. Sure enough, just below the arch of the ceiling, she could see the opening of a passage. It was about four feet across and square in shape.

"Brilliant," Allissa said, a smile breaking across her face. She stepped up close to the wall and extended her arms as high as she could. The hole was about twelve feet above the ground and well out of reach.

Allissa scrambled up on to Leo's back, steadying herself against the wall. Leo helped her up, until she was sitting on his shoulders. Allissa reached up, but her hands still fell short of the opening.

"We're not high enough," she hissed, almost losing balance. Leo wobbled one way and then the other before steadying himself.

"Stand up," Leo said, making a step with his hands.

Allissa struggled upwards, first placing a foot on his raised hands, then onto each of his shoulders. Leo grunted with the movement. Allissa stood slowly, walking her hands up along the rough stones. Towards the ceiling, the stone became dry and dusty. She reached her full height and extended her arms above her head. Her fingertips flailed around two inches below the lip of the passage.

"We're so close." Allissa strained herself. Leo pushed up onto his tip toes, the muscles in his feet and legs straining to gain every inch possible. Allissa gritted her teeth and jumped. Her fingertips scrambled against the rock, sending a cloud of dust out into the room. Shards of stone dug beneath her nails. Her fingers slipped and she slid down the wall, Leo catching her before she fell into the water.

"An inch more and I would have made it," Allissa said, catching her breath.

Leo looked around, searching for something that could give the extra elevation.

A crack and splash echoed through the cistern. Another of the stones holding back the flow of water disintegrated and collapsed. The torrent became a deluge, roaring into the cistern. The water spun and swirled at such a pace it was difficult to stand up.

Leo charged across to the desk on which Ramiz's computers had sat. The desk was submerged, but the top edge of the giant monitors were still visible. The water was up to Leo's elbows now. He half swam, half walked, thanking himself for the time he'd spent learning to swim last year.

He crashed into the desk, unable to see it in the turbulent water. One of the monitors disappeared beneath the waves. A shock of pain jarred through his leg, but Leo ignored it. He reached down, grabbed hold of the table, and yanked. It didn't move. He tried again, pulling as hard as he could. His fingers slipped across the surface beneath the water.

"It's not moving," he shouted to Allissa. "It must be bolted down or wedged here somehow."

Leo tried again. His hands slipped, and he tripped, falling into the water. His feet skidded against the stones as he struggled to get his head above the water. A long second passed. Leo's lungs cried for air. His hands fought furiously against swirling waves. Eventually he found his footing, stood up straight, and his head broke free. He took a deep lungful of air. Water lapped against his neck. He looked back across the cistern. Allissa bobbed above the maelstrom on the far side.

Half swimming, half walking, Leo struggled across the room.

When he was still a few feet from Allissa another noise reverberated through the cistern — a dull click. And then, all at once, as though someone had simply cut the cord, the lights went out.

55

Esin rummaged in the cupboard beneath the sink and pulled out a dustpan and brush. She stood and looked around the small kitchen. The coffee machine ticked and bubbled, and the fridge in the corner buzzed noisily. Esin couldn't help but notice how outdated the place was — the walls were discoloured, the counter chipped. A damp patch in the far corner threatened to spread across the whole ceiling.

When they landed this contract, an office makeover would be one of the first things she actioned. No, Esin thought, she would move them out of this old office all together. Somewhere new, bright and modern. Set to be one of the biggest companies in the country, they needed an office space to match.

Striding back towards her office, Esin remembered how Sadik had rejected the call to move out to Ümraniye along with many of the city's biggest businesses. Sadik always said that he wanted the company to stay close to its roots. It was a company for the people, worked on by the people.

What an idiot, Esin thought, pushing through her office

door. A company for the people — now that was a recipe for disaster.

Esin crouched down and swept the broken glass into the dustpan. When the floor was clear, she picked up the frame and looked at the photograph. Shadows fell across Sadik's smiling face.

The phone on the desk behind her trilled, pulling Esin from her thoughts. Still holding the photograph, she strode across the office and answered the call. Burak's voice came down the line. It sounded as though he was driving.

"It has been dealt with," he said gruffly.

"Good," Esin replied. "Get back here. We move out soon."

"Yes boss," Burak said. "I have someone with me I think you'd like to meet."

56

The darkness was like nothing Allissa had ever experienced. A complete and utter surrounding blackness. It was so thick, it seemed as though she could just push it aside.

The water was above her head height now. She kicked, treading water. She turned and extended her arms. The wall was just beside her. Water splashed up on all sides — cold and black. The rough stones cut at her fingers. Her heart pounded.

Her feet kicked freely, backwards and forwards, keeping her afloat. She scraped around, looking for the passage. The circling maelstrom of water dragged her this way and that. She fought her way back to what she assumed was her starting position. She worried that if the current moved her away from the passage, they may not be able to find it again. She couldn't let that happen. It was their only chance.

Allissa dug her fingers into a gap between the stones and listened to the sounds around her. With no sight to go on, sound was everything. All she could hear was the white-noise howl of the water.

Wait, was that splash movement on the other side of the cistern?

She turned towards the noise, willing her ears to discern the individual sounds.

As the water level in the cistern increased, the torrential wail of the falling water lessened slightly. There was another movement. A splashing, on the far side. Instinctively, Allissa turned towards it, losing her handhold for a moment.

"Leo," she shouted, spitting water from her mouth. "Leo, I'm over here. Head towards my voice."

Allissa spat water again and listened for a reply. She kicked harder still, attempting to stay near the passage. She sucked in a deep breath of cold wet air.

She turned to the wall again and ran her fingers upwards across the stones, searching for the passageway. She tried to calculate the pace of the falling water and the distance they had to cover. It would come into reach soon, providing she was still in the right place.

A frantic splashing reverberated through the cistern again, closer this time.

Allissa leaned towards the noise. "Head towards my voice," she shouted again. The splashing continued. For a moment, she remembered Leo, learning to swim in St Lucia several months ago. He had been completely against the idea, but Allissa had insisted after he'd almost drowned in Hong Kong. Practising in the pool, he had become more confident. He could now tread water and pull off some basic strokes without panicking. Allissa hoped he'd remembered their training now.

"Head this way," she yelled again, pushing her back against the wall. "We'll be out of here soon."

Allissa turned and ran her fingers against the stones. The crack she'd used to steady herself was now far below the water level. They were rising quickly. She extended her arms as far as she could. Her fingers grasped the edge of the passage above her. Relief washed over her. That was their chance of escape. Her fingers, numb from the cold, curled around the edge of the stone.

She kicked harder, forcing herself upwards and out of the water. Her fingers slid further into the space. She tried to hold on, to grip something, but the stone here was worn smooth. The muscles in her legs burned like acid and her heart pounded harder than the torrent behind her. She slid both hands right and left, looking for something to grasp. Nothing. There was nothing there. An empty space. Her muscles burned, begging to be allowed to rest. Allissa pushed harder, expending all the energy she had, looking for something to grasp.

Allissa's fingers slid into a fissure in the stone a few inches from the lip. She dug her fingertips hard into the crack and heaved herself up. She dragged her body, like a dead weight, from the water. Her arms shook and buckled. Her fingertips scratched against the rock. She tensed every muscle, grimaced, pulled herself clear of the water, and up onto the ledge.

A cool breath of night air drifted across the back of her neck. Allissa picked up the vague saline scent of the sea. They weren't far. She turned around to face into the cistern, sat on the ledge, and let the cool air of freedom slide into her lungs.

57

"Leo, where are you?" Allissa shouted. When she'd hauled herself up on the ledge, the water had been beneath her feet. Now it was around her ankles.

Allissa stared into the dark passage, willing her eyes to pick something up. The passage was dark, but the faint breeze brought with it the scent of the outside. She turned back towards the turbulent sloshing of the cistern. Leo was somewhere in there. The thought wrenched at her chest.

"We need to go now," Allissa yelled, her voice cracking. "I can't go without you. Come towards my voice, please." Her voice wobbled with undisguised fear. "Now. We need to go now!" Allissa leaned out from the ledge and listened in to the sounds reverberating around the cistern. The splashes had stopped now. She hated to think what that could mean.

The water crept insidiously up towards her knees. Once it reached the ledge it would pour, unstoppable, down the passage, possibly blocking their exit.

Allissa turned to the passage behind her. Warm air from the outside streamed across her face. Maybe she should go out there and get help. She could contact the emergency services and be back here in a few minutes. If Leo could hold on that long.

She tried to swallow, but her throat constricted. Her stomach bubbled and writhed with the thought. She couldn't leave Leo, but she couldn't keep waiting, either.

"Leo," Allissa wailed. "Where are you? We need to go! Come here!" She gripped the edge of the passage, the stone worn smooth beneath her palms. Allissa had sworn many times that she wouldn't leave Leo's side, and he had sworn the same. They faced things together. As a team they had found success when all seemed lost, and survived when every odd was stacked against them.

Allissa turned towards the passage. She took a deep breath of the outside air.

"I don't…" she stuttered. "I don't want to have to leave you. I can't leave you."

The water slipped higher still. It covered Allissa's fingers now, just an inch below the ledge.

She scrunched her eyes closed and tensed the muscles in her arms.

"I can't leave you, but I can't stay either," she whispered, realisation flooding her. "I'm going to have to —"

Allissa's voice caught in her throat as a hand closed around her ankle. Her heart froze mid-beat.

Leo croaked somewhere in the darkness, his voice constricted with barely controlled panic. "Help me up."

58

Leo scrambled, his muscles drained of energy, up into the passage. Allissa pulled him by the arm. He shivered uncontrollably. Water poured from his clothes.

"We need to get out of here," Allissa said. Her voice breathless in the darkness. The water rose above the level of the passage and trickled down across the floor.

Leo and Allissa struggled to their feet, using the walls for support. The passage was perhaps four feet wide and five feet tall. Leo stood bent over, his shoulders touching the passageway's low roof. He extended his arms and pushed against the walls to balance himself.

"This way," Allissa said, her voice loud in the narrow space. She extended a hand towards Leo. "Keep close to me. I don't think it's far."

Another gust of wind pushed through the passage. The smell of the outside world was tantalisingly close.

Allissa set off as quickly as she could, feeling the direction of the passage with her hands against the walls. After a few steps, they descended at a steep angle.

Allissa slowed further. She placed each foot carefully in

front of the other, holding her breath each time. Centuries of flowing water had worn the floor into smooth rivulets — like veins beneath skin.

They picked their way forward, checking each foot would hold before committing to it.

Water bubbled and rushed across the stones beneath their feet, making the journey even more treacherous.

The level rose further, the water streaming above her ankles now.

A deep rumble vibrated the passageway. It growled and groaned, shaking the water around them. The temperature dropped a few degrees. Allissa shuddered.

"What's that?" Leo hissed, his voice tremulous.

"I don't —" The grip of their hands broke.

A sudden increase in the water level caught Allissa off guard. She jammed her hands into the walls as the water rose to the level of her knees. The rocks cut against her palms.

"Water," Leo shouted. "Something must have collapsed back there."

Allissa pushed her hands harder into the walls on either side, wedging herself still. The water pushed powerfully against her legs, loosening their grip. She felt the pressure tearing, ripping at the back of her legs.

Another boom resounded through the ancient structure, shaking Allissa to the core.

"Take a deep breath," Leo shouted from somewhere behind her. His voice was almost lost against the howling noise. "Let go when the next wave hits you."

Allissa tried to pull a deep breath, but the air was filled was spraying, furious water. She coughed, the air knocked clean from her lungs.

It felt like a collision with a juggernaut. Allissa's hands

scrabbled against the sides of the passage. Her skin scraped across the rugged stones. Water roared in her ears, deafening her. Then she was moving forwards, twisting and turning, thrown this way and that. She spun one way, then the other. She lost all sense of direction, and speed.

Allissa pulled her arms and legs in close to her body, increasing her speed. She resisted the urge to breathe, knowing only water surrounded them now. Her lungs stung with the pain of inactivity. Every synapse begged to inhale.

The torrent pushed her on. Distant bangs and crashes reverberated directly into her saturated ear drums.

Her lungs seared some more, burning with the desire to breathe. She focused in, trying to listen and make sense of what was around her. The movement around her started to slow, or was it speeding up? She couldn't be sure. She pulled herself tighter into a ball. Her body burned. Her muscles seared. Then her vision filled with light. Bright light. The most beautiful bright light she'd ever seen.

59

Something struck Leo's back, hard. The impact knocked the last ravages of air from his lungs with an explosive cough. He resisted the urge to breathe. It would be futile. If he took a breath water would stream into his lungs, clogging him, filling him, preventing him from ever breathing again. His chest burned, as though it had been filled with molten iron. Then, instinct took over.

He pulled cold, delicious air in through his nose and mouth. It slipped easily into his lungs.

Leo opened his eyes in surprise. The night sky stretched above him, backed by the orange glow of the city. Leo extended his arms and felt solid ground surround him. He dug his fingers into it. He took another breath. This one came even easier than the last, although his lungs and throat ached.

He heard a coughing, spluttering noise from somewhere nearby.

"Allissa!" he yelled, his voice sounding distant against the water swirling in his ears.

He rolled over, his muscles protesting at the movement.

Allissa lay beside him, wheezing and coughing water onto the ground.

He blinked a few times, and his eyes pulled into focus. From the dull, ambient light of the sky, Leo saw that they lay on a slab of concrete beside the ocean. Either side of them, the shoreline consisted of giant concrete cubes. The sea made a great sucking, whooshing noise as it moved between them. Leo glanced behind. A dozen feet away the mouth of the passage yawned. The water had now reduced to a small trickle, which ran past them down the concrete and into the ocean.

Allissa spat the last bit of water from her lungs and sat up. She looked down at her hands. Cuts littered her palms.

"You're hurt," Leo said, shuffling beside her.

"I'm fine," she said. "They've almost stopped bleeding already."

Allissa looked out at the water before them. The lights of Istanbul's Asian side glittered and danced on the inky surface.

Leo pulled another deep breath. He tilted his head one way, and then the other. Pain stabbed through his neck with each movement. The water in his ears popped, then drained away. He listened to the distant grumble of the city, the slurp and swoosh of the waves, the deep groan of a nearby engine.

Slowly, Leo came out of his daze, and the images of what had just happened scrolled through his mind. The cistern, the darkness, the rising water. He tried to speak, but the words caught in his throat.

Allissa turned. Her hair hung down her back. Her face was devoid of emotion. She looked exhausted. She clearly didn't have the words to express what had happened either.

Leo put his arms around Allissa and nestled his face into her shoulder. Allissa did the same. The warmth of her body moved into his. Slowly, incrementally, his heartrate slowed and his breathing normalised. A shiver moved collectively through their connected bodies.

Then, just for a moment, they were illuminated in a dazzling white light. The light disappeared, leaving colours dancing across Leo's vision.

"What was that?" Leo raised his head and looked out towards the sea.

A boat cruised slowly towards them. A bright searchlight mounted on the bow swept the surface of the water, encrusting each wave with a crown of jewels.

Leo and Allissa watched the boat, too exhausted to move.

The searchlight swept past them, paused, and then returned, bathing them in stark white light.

Leo looked away, dazzled. He had the vague sensation that maybe they should move. He instructed his legs to get going, but they disobeyed.

Allissa sat silently beside him, looking down at her hands.

The searchlight continued to blaze, unmoving. Leo glanced up at the boat. Colours danced across his vision. The boat changed direction and was now closing in on them. Its shadow merged into focus. The deep *thud thud* of the boat's engine cut through the noise of the water.

Leo again instructed his feet into action. They should leave now. Again, his feet resisted. Every muscle in his body resisted. Allissa shared his reluctance.

A loud whistling sound emanated from the boat, followed by a click. Then a voice spoke over a loudspeaker. Leo heard the voice but didn't make sense of it straight away.

"Are you Leo and Allissa?" the voice said again, almost irritably.

Leo and Allissa looked directly into the blinding light. Leo raised his hand to shield his eyes and nodded. "Yes!" he shouted.

"Where's Ramiz?" Although distorted by the speaker system, Leo could tell the voice was accented and female. It wasn't Burak. Leo found that reassuring.

"They took him away," Leo shouted in reply, unsure if his voice would carry across the water and the growl of the engine.

The voice didn't reply for several moments. "Stay where you are. I'm coming to get you."

The noise of another engine joined the boat's deep growl, this one high pitched. A skiff appeared from the stern of the larger boat and raced across the water. Powered by a small outboard motor, it skipped effortlessly through the waves. The skiff drew up to the edge of the concrete slab, just ten feet from Leo and Allissa. Water from its wake slapped the concrete, wheezing and whooshing through the gaps.

"Get in," came the female voice again.

Leo examined the silhouette of the boat's skipper. She was slight, but precise in her movement. She knew what she was doing.

Leo and Allissa glanced at each other. Leo peered back into the gloom. They had two choices; get on the boat with a stranger, or fend for themselves. Leo listened in to his instincts. He looked towards the skiff, bobbing a few feet away.

"Let's go," Leo said, struggling to his feet. "We can't sit here all night, and I could really do with warming up."

60

The skiff sliced through the water, back towards the imposing hull of the larger boat.

Allissa examined the boat as they neared. It was an executive yacht with a hull in dark blue or black. The upper decks were clad in wood. Most of the windows were dark, except for the bridge, which glowed dully.

Allissa glanced back at the skipper. The young woman swung the skiff adeptly in an ark behind the yacht. Her large waterproof coat rustled as she killed the engine and drew them gently in close to the yacht's stern. The outboard sunk into an idle patter.

Still without a word to Leo and Allissa, the skipper jumped from the skiff to the yacht. She landed skilfully on the back deck and secured the skiff to a pair of large hydraulic arms. Leo and Allissa struggled out of the skiff, their legs still wobbling. They steadied themselves on a railing.

The skipper pressed a button on a hanging remote control. The hydraulic arms pulled the skiff from the water.

"This way," the woman said, fixing Leo and then Allissa

with a stare. Her bright hazel eyes and wide smile softened her face. Allissa paused. A strange pang of recognition moved through it. She had seen this woman somewhere before.

Leo and Allissa followed the woman up a flight of stairs and into the cockpit. The woman shrugged off the waterproof coat and hung it on the door. Her long dark hair, twisted into a thick plait, swung across her back as she crossed the room.

"I know who you are," she said, turning, her hands on her hips. "But I'm aware that you don't yet know me."

The sense of recognition throbbed in Allissa's consciousness again.

"I'm Xanthe." The woman tilted her head to one side and looked from Allissa to Leo. Whilst she appeared to be Turkish, with olive skin and dark hair, her voice had an American intonation. "Ramiz is my brother."

Leo nodded slowly.

"We've seen you before," Allissa said, her voice weak.

"That's correct, I was in the Grand Bazaar." Xanthe now spoke with a thick Turkish accent. "You want fish hall, let me show you." She grinned. "I was in the airport too, but I don't think you saw me. You shouldn't have seen me, anyway."

Leo opened his mouth as though to speak... eventually the words came. "You and Ramiz work together?"

"Something like that, yeah." Xanthe crossed to the yacht's controls. "He's great at all the tech stuff. Get him away from his computer, though, and he's no good to anyone." Xanthe clicked the throttle forwards. The engine gurgled from somewhere far below decks and the yacht slipped through the water. "That's why we're going to have to get him back."

61

As Xanthe navigated the yacht back up the Bosphorus and towards their mooring at Istmarin Marina, Leo and Allissa headed below decks to shower and change.

They returned to the cockpit with an armful of snacks and bottles of beers from the yacht's well stocked kitchen. Leo peered up at the glowing expanse of the Fatih Sultan Mehmet Bridge stretching across the water two hundred feet above them. The pounding tyres of traffic on the Europe to Asia highway was inaudible from here. The bridge appeared to float in the darkness.

"Feel better?" Xanthe said, turning from the controls and flashing them a smile.

"So much," Leo said, taking a gulp from a cold bottle of beer and then stuffing a handful of crisps in his mouth. "I can't believe... I'm still trying..." his voice trailed off as the sensation of the dark cold water lapped across his memory.

"How did you know where we were?" Allissa said, taking a ravenous bite from a chocolate bar.

"There's a silent alarm in the cistern. Ramiz must have activated it before he was taken. We'd always agreed that if he got into trouble down there, he would use the passage down to the Bosphorus. I didn't expect you to flood the place, though."

"Sorry about that," Leo mumbled. "We couldn't help it... sort of."

"He's been working down there for years. I think he had the impression that it was so off-grid no one would ever find it. I kept telling him to be careful, that one of these days they'd track him there, but he wouldn't listen." Xanthe's voice turned wistful. She spun the wheel, pulling them from the wake of a large freighter gliding the other way.

"How long has he been doing this?" Allissa asked.

"Ever since our father..." Xanthe's voice trailed off. She cleared her throat. "Ever since our father died, Ramiz has taken it on himself to be some kind of warrior for the truth. I keep telling him that you can't take on everyone, but he never listens."

Allissa watched the blood drain from Xanthe's knuckles. The freighter passed and the glassy black surface of the water settled down. Xanthe swung them back out into the centre of the waterway.

"How long ago did your father die?" Allissa asked, her voice taking on a soft tone.

"Just over ten years. His car ran off the road, up in the mountains. We were just teenagers at the time. The newspapers reported he was driving drunk, but Ramiz and I know that wasn't true. Our father never touched a drop. That's where Ramiz's crusade to stop the media telling lies came from, I think."

Allissa nodded. She thought about her own father. Whist he wasn't dead, she hadn't seen him since the trial, during which her testimony had sent him to prison. The man she'd known as her father had long since gone. Not dead, but corrupted by greed and violence.

"He'd left us his share of his business in his estate, but before we'd even finished grieving the other shareholders forced us to sell. One of them, a woman called Esin Kartan, did everything she could to discredit our father, just to get the business for herself. There was nothing we could do other than sell to them. I mean, we've never wanted for anything. I can't complain about that, but that business was his life."

"What did your father do?"

"He was a scientist, of sorts. His company created life-saving technology for health organisations. Devices that monitor vital signs, deliver medicines, that sort of thing. He even created a machine that can automatically restart the heart if the patient has a cardiac arrest."

The Istmarin Marina appeared on the left bank of the river. Rows of yachts bobbed gently in the water. Xanthe swung the wheel and slowed the engine.

"I'm sorry to hear that. He sounds like a great man," Leo said, demolishing one packet of crisps and instantly opening a second.

Xanthe smiled weakly. She clicked the engine into its lowest register and the yacht slowed to a crawl.

"He was," Xanthe said, pulling them alongside the pontoon. "That's why we have to get Ramiz back and stop this madness."

"Where do we start?" Leo said.

Xanthe jumped up onto the pier. "Follow me," she replied, smiling through the sadness.

62

"It is done," Burak said, shoving Ramiz forwards into Esin's office.

Ramiz stumbled into the room, his hands taped behind his back and a sack pulled down across his face. He lurched around, twisting left and right. Although he'd spent the journey trying to work out where they were going, he had no idea.

"Have you totally lost your mind?" Esin asked, climbing to her feet.

Burak took a step backwards, and then looked up at his boss.

Esin pointed a long finger at the prisoner. "I told you to get rid of them. Get them locked up, send them home, kill them. I don't really care. But I didn't want you to bring them here. What are we supposed to do now?"

The only lights in the office were the glowing screen of the television and the turbulent illumination of the city seven floors below. Somewhere nearby a siren shrieked and then faded. Another night of violent protests was coming to an end.

"You don't understand, boss —"

"I think I do understand," Esin spat, interrupting Burak and marching around the table, her hands on her hips. "You're the one who hasn't understood the most basic of instructions. Get rid of the detectives — how hard can it be?"

"No." Burak glanced at Ramiz, who was struggling to stand up. "He's not one of the detectives. This man is responsible for all this," Burak said, pointing at Ramiz.

"Yes, so why is he not dead like the others? Instead, you bring him here? Get rid of him! Now!"

"I thought maybe you'd like a word with him, for old time's sake," Burak said, a mysterious grin lighting his face. He pulled off the sack.

It took Esin a few moments to realise what Burak was talking about. She looked from Ramiz to the photograph on her desk. Her eyes widened, and her hands fell to her sides.

"It's you," she said, pacing towards him. "You have caused us a lot of trouble."

63

Leo and Allissa, wearing thick bathrobes while their clothes spun in the tumble drier, sunk into the sofa in the yacht's main living area. Allissa looked down the row of vessels tied to the floating walkway. Xanthe's was one of the largest here. Most of the other boats sat in darkness.

"She's a cool lady, right?" Allissa said, watching Xanthe tie the yacht securely in place and then leap back on board. She landed soundlessly on the back deck and padded inside.

Xanthe pressed a button on the wall and electronic curtains buzzed closed.

"How many gadgets does this boat have?" Leo asked.

"A lot," Xanthe replied, smiling. "You've met my brother, right?"

Xanthe pulled out a laptop and settled into the other sofa. Her fingers flew over the keys. "Ramiz sent me a video just before he raised the alarm."

Leo and Allissa glanced at each other.

"We were watching Brent Fasslane's disappearance just

as those men arrived," Allissa said. Leo munched furiously on his third packet of crisps.

Xanthe tapped the keyboard. A wooden panel slid aside, revealing a screen built into the wall. The video started to play.

Xanthe placed the laptop on the coffee table.

The police vehicle cut through the streets, the drone following from several hundred feet above. The truck reached an intersection and turned left.

Leo, Allissa and Xanthe watched in silence. The truck turned onto a dual carriageway and sped up. The drone lagged behind for a few seconds before accelerating quickly.

Leo glanced at Xanthe, relaxing into the sofa.

The truck slowed and turned off the dual carriageway.

Xanthe suddenly jolted upright. Her hands rose slowly to cover her face.

The truck pulled down a side street, paused and then turned into the underground car park of an office building.

Leo and Allissa looked at Xanthe. Her face was a mask of shock. She pointed at the screen, unable to speak.

"What is it? What have you seen?" Allissa said, rushing to her side.

"That's... that's..." Xanthe stuttered. "That's the offices of my father's company."

64

For several seconds Xanthe stared at the screen without moving. The drone hovered, filming the building into which the police truck had disappeared.

Other than the Sadik-Tech logo, which glowed above the door, the building was dark.

The video cut out and the screen faded to black.

Xanthe put her head in her hands. No one spoke for a few seconds. When Xanthe raised her head, her mouth was set in a determined frown. Her eyes burned with something close to fury.

"I don't understand why the company would be involved in this." Xanthe looked from the screen to Allissa and Leo. "Last I heard, they were involved in something for the government. No idea what business they would have with" — she pointed at the screen — "what's his name?"

"Brent Fasslane," Allissa said, explaining who he was and the issues he'd caused.

Xanthe listened closely, and then summarised. "Basically, the Turkish government think it's the Americans, the

Americans think it's the Turkish, meanwhile everyone else thinks it's a sign that the stuff in his book is true."

"Exactly," Leo said. "His disappearance is causing a lot of issues."

"I can see why my brother's involved," Xanthe said. "It's exactly the sort of thing he would get behind, particularly if it involves Sadik-Tech."

The three fell into silence again. The yacht bobbed forwards and backwards on a swell. The air conditioner hummed gently.

Allissa and Leo exchanged a glance. Leo's Adam's apple bobbed and he nodded almost imperceptibly.

"We need to go and get your brother," Allissa said.

"If we find Ramiz, there's a good change we will find Fasslane too," Leo said, trying to force a steady tone into his voice.

Xanthe's large eyes slid from Allissa to Leo and then to the laptop on the table. For several moment she didn't move, her face clouded with thought. Then she grabbed the laptop and tapped at the keyboard. A building's blueprint appeared on the screen. The document showed the buildings layout, including points of entry and exit.

"What are you looking at?" Allissa asked.

"After my dad died, I saved all of his files. Something told me they might be useful one day."

"This is the building on the —" Leo pointed at the screen.

"Correct. On the seventh floor are the executive offices. That's where my father's office was, and that of his leading team. There are meeting rooms too, that sort of thing. He even installed an area for people to rest and shower if they needed it."

"And you think —" Leo started, but didn't get to finish his sentence.

"I bet you that's where Fasslane is," Xanthe said. "My dad used to boast that the place had everything you need without setting foot outside. Gym, cinema room, snacks. He provided all that sort of thing for the people who worked there."

Another blueprint appeared on the screen. This one detailed the layout of a particular floor. Leo looked at it closely; it seemed more like a luxury apartment than a commercial building.

"This elevator" — Xanthe pointed at the screen — "only goes between the seventh floor and the parking garage beneath the building."

"That means people could arrive and leave without being seen, right?" Leo asked.

"Exactly. We need to go in there, get my brother and find out what's happening with Fasslane." Xanthe stood and paced to the window. She pulled one of the curtains aside and peered out. "And we need to do it tonight."

Leo and Alissa glanced at each other.

Xanthe turned. "Listen, I can do it alone, you've risked at lot today –"

"No way," Leo and Allissa interrupted in unison.

"If it wasn't for Ramiz, there's no knowing where we'd be," Allissa said, standing. "We're not leaving him in there for a moment longer than necessary."

65

"If only your father could see you now," Esin said, pacing across the office and staring down at Ramiz. Burak had tied the man to a chair. It hardly seemed necessary, as the young man hadn't tried to fight or struggle at all. His large hazel-coloured eyes looked up helplessly at Esin.

"You're pathetic. Look at yourself now. You sit, day after day, behind the screen of your computer, causing issues for us all. You think you're this big guy with all these answers. Making the world a better place. Ha!" Esin leaned in so that her face was just inches from Ramiz. "Now look at you. You're an embarrassment."

Standing at the door, Burak shifted his weight from one foot to the other. He watched Esin and Ramiz closely.

"Your father was the same I suppose. He was a coward too, right up until the end."

Esin turned and examined Ramiz closely. Ramiz blinked several times, his eyes watery. It looked to Esin as though he were about to cry. For a moment Esin considered what it must feel like to care about someone that deeply. She forced the thought from her mind and steeled her expression.

"You know, I could kill you, right now, just like that. I could even take you out to that same stretch of mountain road and send you off down the cliff. No one would even ask any questions — a troubled young man, still mourning the loss of his father."

Ramiz blinked twice. He swallowed.

"I could do that, right now, just like that." Esin snapped her fingers.

Burak pulled his gun from the holster.

Ramiz didn't move. He continued staring up at Esin, now unblinking.

Esin beckoned for Burak to approach. Burak did as he was told, gun raised.

Ramiz glanced at Burak, approaching. He swallowed, but still said nothing.

Burak levelled the gun at Ramiz's head.

Ramiz took a deep breath, his chest swelling. He remained silent.

"But what would be the point?" Esin growled. "There's a certain glory in death."

Esin exhaled and turned towards the window.

"No, I think you're better alive, at least for now. That way you'll continue to be an embarrassment to your family name."

Esin turned to Burak. "We'll leave him here. A couple of nights locked to that chair will do him good."

66

Xanthe's all electric Toyota BZ4X whispered down the fast lane of the dual carriageway, overtaking a lumbering truck which spewed clouds of smoke into the already saturated city air.

Reclining in the passenger seat, Leo examined the controls. Details about their location, speed, and the running of the vehicle showed on a large screen in the centre console. Beside him, Xanthe gripped the tiny steering wheel, which looked to Leo like something from a fighter jet. Leo turned back to the screen and looked at the clock — it was quickly approaching 2am. He tried to piece together the events of the day.

Only twelve hours had passed since their mysterious meeting at the Grand Bazaar. It felt like days ago. He stifled a yawn and glanced at Allissa in the back seat. She looked tired too.

The Sea of Marmara stretched out to their left, murky and featureless. Only the tankers which waited at anchor, or sluggishly pushed through the oil-coloured night, their lights spewing across the water, broke the monotony of the night.

Xanthe slowed and swung the Toyota up a slip road. Without slowing her speed, she took a right, then a left turn. Lightweight tyres screeched across the asphalt. Restaurants and shops flashed past, all shut up for the night. Metal shutters covered the windows of some, others were boarded up against the violence and protests that had swept through the city.

Dozens of signs in countless languages shouted for attention.

The Toyota screeched around a T-junction. Leo glanced anxiously to the right. He was glad to see the road was empty. Parked cars lay dormant on each side of the carriageway. Two had their windscreens smashed in and lay charred by flames.

The occasional light glowed from concrete apartment buildings on either side of the road. Most windows were unlit.

If you wanted to smuggle something or someone out of the city, this would be the perfect time to do it, Leo thought.

The Toyota accelerated further, pinning Leo into the seat. He glanced at the speedometer. The digital display climbed past eighty. Leo looked at Xanthe as the amber glow of a streetlight swept across her face. Her jaw was locked forward in an expression of steely resolve. Her eyes swept the road before them.

Leo knew how it felt to protect a sibling. A few months ago, Leo's brother-in-law had gone missing in New York and Leo's sister, distraught and panicked, had called them in to help. The case had been dangerous, and painfully personal for Leo.

The Toyota screeched into a side street.

"Short cut," Xanthe shouted.

Metal stairwells zigzagged up discoloured concrete walls on either side. Washing, stiff and forgotten, hung between the buildings, swaying slowly in the breeze. They cruised past several overflowing bins. A family of tabby cats examined the silent vehicle from behind piles of rubbish.

"We're going to find him, you know?" Leo said, his voice loud against the silent vehicle. "There's no need to worry about that at all."

Xanthe's eyes flicked from the road to Leo. She smiled weakly and lessened her pressure on the accelerator.

"He's the only family I've got," Xanthe said after a few seconds' silence.

Leo nodded. "You're not losing him tonight."

"And we're going to solve this," Allissa said, as they passed a restaurant, its windows smashed. "We need to expose this guy for the fraud he is."

Leo nodded.

"I hope so," Xanthe said, looking forlorn. "I really hope so..." Her voice trailed off, before she yelled, "There it is!"

She swung the Toyota around a tight corner. Leo peered up at the glass and concrete building. Set back from the road, and fronted by a wide, grand plaza, the tower occupied the entire city block. Whilst it was only seven storeys in height, it dwarfed its neighbours.

"I thought you said it had sea views?" Leo said, looking around. They were surrounded on all sides by a jumble of mismatched buildings.

"You can from the seventh floor." Xanthe pointed towards the upper floors. "My father resisted the pressure to move to Ümraniye as the business grew. He saw this as his home, as well as that of the business.

Xanthe slowed the Toyota and turned towards the

underground car park. Above them, the Sadik-Tech sign glowed. Hovering in the darkness, the red logo was strangely menacing.

The Toyota swept down the ramp and into the underground car park. Xanthe momentarily slowed the Toyota as a horizontal barrier came into view. Then, with a grumble, she stamped on the accelerator. The Toyota leapt forward. The barrier snapped clean off and skittered across the car park.

"Won't they know we're coming?" Allissa hissed from the back seat.

"Maybe," Xanthe said, slamming the Toyota to a stop. The tyres screeched. She killed the lights and climbed out of the car.

Leo and Allissa scrambled out too. Allissa glanced at Xanthe. Wearing black sports clothes, Allissa couldn't help but compare the young woman to a character in an action movie. She certainly was fearless enough to play the role.

Xanthe opened the boot and rummaged around inside. "I don't care if they know we're coming," she said, distracted. "I'm ready."

67

Esin studied Ramiz one more time. The small man sat upright in the chair in the middle of her office. The city smouldered behind him through the window. Only the thick bands of several strong cable ties binding his ankles and wrists to the chair indicated that he wasn't merely resting.

Burak had added more for reinforcement a minute ago. Esin had instructed him to yank the ties until they pinched Ramiz's skin. Ramiz was not going anywhere.

Esin smiled and caught the man's eye. To her frustration, Ramiz hadn't pleaded, complained or even muttered a single word since entering the office. The small man was tougher than she would like to admit.

"Enjoy yourself," Esin said, smiling and crossing to the door. "We'll be back in two days, maybe three. I think that should give you enough time to re-evaluate your life decisions."

Ramiz looked up at her from the chair, his expression blank. Then, like a tropical flower opening in the spring, he grinned.

Rage rose through Esin's body. She fought to force it down. She would have all the time she wanted to deal with him later. She slammed the door, sending the brass sign into fits of vibration, then pulled the key from her pocket and locked it.

We'll see if he's still smiling in three days' time, Esin thought, trying the handle. It was securely locked. Even if, by some miracle, he managed to get out of the bindings, he wouldn't get out of the room.

Feet thundered down the corridor. Esin turned to see Burak running towards her, a tablet in his hands.

"Boss, boss, someone's coming," Burak shouted, thrusting the tablet towards her. "This happened two minutes ago."

On the screen a car careered into the car park, smashing the barrier to the side. The car squealed to a stop and three people got out. Recognising them, Esin's face turned to rage.

"We get out of here now. We'll pass them in the lift." Esin's eyes locked on Burak's. "You've failed me again. I'll deal with you later."

"What about him?" Burak pointed towards the office.

Esin looked at the door and thought for a moment. If they left him here, he would be found and rescued. If they took him with them there was the chance he could escape, and travelling with one more person would slow them down. There seemed to be only one option.

"Kill him," Esin said, her eyes locking on Burak's. Her voice was toneless.

The big man's Adam's Apple bobbed.

"Put a bullet in his brain so there's no doubt." Esin forced the key into Burak's thick hand. "Don't let me down this time, okay?"

A single bead of sweat ran down Burak's forehead. He wiped it away, then nodded once.

68

Xanthe strode to rear of the Toyota and opened the boot. A light snapped on. She rummaged through a black rucksack and extracted three heavy-duty torches. She gave Leo and Allissa one each, then swung the rucksack onto her back.

"Is this all we've got?" Allissa said, looking at the torch. "They'll have guns up there."

Leo weighed up the torch and thought about how they'd faced people with guns before and survived. Hopefully today would be no exception.

"Yep," Xanthe said, slamming the boot closed. "My father was against weapons. We have everything we need here." She tapped the side of her head. "Keep the lights off for now. Follow me."

Xanthe led them deeper into the carpark. Darkness swamped large areas of the underground space. A fluorescent bulb flickered on the far side, casting strange and wraithlike shadows across the concrete.

Several vehicles, including the police van, two armoured vehicles and a couple of luxury civilian cars, sat against the far wall.

Xanthe paused and dug a phone from her pocket. One of the building's schematics filled the screen. Her fingers darted around, finding the part she required. "This way," she said finally, leading them on.

Xanthe reached a door in the far corner.

Danger electricity. Do not enter, read a sign in Turkish, and below in English.

Xanthe twisted the handle and pulled. The door shuddered against its fixings but didn't open.

"No matter," Xanthe muttered, pulling the bag from her back. She rummaged around inside and removed a small crowbar.

"That could totally be used as a weapon," Leo said sarcastically.

"No, this is a tool," Xanthe retorted, grinning. She shoved the bar between the door and the frame, then heaved it with surprising force. The door popped free of its lock. Xanthe snapped on the torch. A large array of electrical equipment blinked from the far wall of a small room. She strode over to the master breaker and pulled down the switch. A dull clang resonated through the room. The building fell into total darkness.

69

Esin pressed the button beside the express lift which would take them straight down to the car park. There was of course a chance that the intruders would still be down there when they arrived. In a way, she hoped they were. A bullet in each of them would be a fitting end.

The screen above the door displayed a number six — the lift was on the floor below. Behind the doors, the system whirred and hummed for a few moments. Then the doors strained open. Esin and Fasslane stepped inside. Esin glanced at Fasslane in the lift's mirrored wall. His face was twisted into an angry frown. He looked as though this was all a big inconvenience for him. A fissure of anger moved through her. With everything she was doing for him, the fame, the fortune, the glory, the least he could do was be civil.

Esin turned and looked out at the seventh floor. The door to her office stood open — what was Burak doing in there? It shouldn't take more than a few seconds.

As though in answer to her question, a gunshot rang

through the office. It was followed by a dull thump. Then silence.

The lift doors tried to close. Esin leaned forwards and forced them to stay open.

Burak appeared from her office, the gun still in his hand. His face hung, gaunt and expressionless.

"Is it done?" Esin asked.

Burak stepped into the lift and slid his gun into the holster at his hip. He nodded once.

"Good." Esin pressed the button and the lift doors slid closed. The mechanism clunked, tapped, and they started to descend.

Esin watched the numbers on the screen begin their count down. She thought of Ramiz, bleeding out on the floor of her office. She would deal with that in a couple of days. It was nothing that couldn't be hushed up if you knew the right people. In fact, she could even pin it on the British detectives. She had video evidence of them entering the building, after all. The idea began to take shape in her mind.

A loud click reverberated through the lift. The lights snapped off, plunging them into complete darkness. The lift ground to a halt.

"They've killed the electricity," Esin snarled. Her voice sounded loud in the enclosed space.

An emergency light clicked on and filled the lift in a soft orange glow. Esin glanced at the men either side of her.

"The emergency generators will fire up in a few seconds."

70

"This way," Xanthe said, leading them back across the car park. A couple of emergency lights shone from near the exits, the rest of the floor lay shrouded in darkness.

Leo clicked on his torch. A finger of light swept through the space and rested on a set of double doors at the far end.

They doubled their pace towards the doors and pushed through into a stairwell.

"Why aren't these doors locked?" Alissa asked, looking at the mag-lock system mounted at the top of each door.

"No power," Xanthe said, grinning. "It looks like they haven't upgraded since my father died. This company isn't as profitable as it appears. Seventh floor."

Xanthe led them up the stairs. Their footsteps hammered on the bare concrete floors. Pipes and electrical cables ran up the walls. Aside from the three fingers of light, sweeping haphazardly from their torches, the darkness was absolute.

Leo's pulse quickened with the climb. As fit as he was, by the fifth floor his heart flung itself against his ribs.

On the sixth floor, Xanthe paused. She leaned over the railing and looked up at the floor above them.

Leo caught his breath and tried to quell the rising, sickening sense of unease. He peered through the glass panel on the door into the sixth floor. Two or three emergency lights were the only distinguishable features.

"I remember coming here as a child," Xanthe said, as Allissa caught up, panting. "My father's team used to treat us like celebrities. They'd spoil us, take turns in looking after us. Back then, I thought they were just nice people. That all changed after he died."

"People can be two faced," Allissa said, catching her breath. "Especially when money's involved."

A motor whirred somewhere in the building. It was almost indistinguishable above the distant whispering traffic.

"What's that?" Leo asked, his torch sweeping the stairwell.

"Not sure," Xanthe whispered. "Let's keep going. Quietly."

Refreshed from the pause, the three charged up the stairwell to the seventh floor. Xanthe reached the landing a few steps ahead of the others. She peered through the door's glass panel. The floor, like those below, was unlit.

Leo and Allissa joined her a moment later.

The three stood stationary, listening.

"I can't hear anything," Allissa said. "If Ramiz is here then —"

Xanthe charged forwards, panic etched across her face.

"We go in together," Allissa said, grabbing Xanthe by the arm. "We have no idea what we're going to find in there."

Xanthe pulled a deep breath, her muscles tense.

"You're no good to anyone dead," Leo said, instantly regretting his harsh word choice. "Let's go, in three, two…"

They charged through the door together, senses on high alert. Leo took two steps, panned out to the left, and paused. His torch swept the room in front of him. As Xanthe had described, it was sumptuously furnished. Fashionable leather sofas squatted in the dimness. Large plants cast strange shadows in the torchlight. Downtown Istanbul glowed through the windows, the inky blanket of the sea beyond.

Xanthe pushed forward into the middle of the space. Allissa scurried over to the right. Their torch beams swept erratically over desks and chairs.

The whole building was as silent as a grave.

Leo reached a row of doors. Executive offices, he assumed, by the brass plaques glimmering from the wood.

"In here, maybe," Leo whispered. He approached the first door and depressed the handle. The mechanism clicked. The door wasn't locked.

Leo took a deep breath. His pulse thundered in his ears. He tried not to think about what might be inside. Leo steeled himself, muscles tensed, and pushed the door open.

The door creaked and swung inwards.

Leo stepped inside. He panned his torch around the office. The room was empty. More than empty though, Leo thought; the place looked unused. There were no photographs on the desks, no papers in trays, no books on the shelves.

He exhaled and stepped back into the outer office.

Leo tried the next three doors. All the executive offices were empty and abandoned.

Approaching the last door, Leo was joined by Allissa and Xanthe.

"Anything?" he asked.

Both shook their heads.

"The place is empty," Allissa whispered. "It's like no one's been here in ages."

Leo nodded.

Leo, Allissa and Xanthe raised their torches. Three beams of light converged on the final door.

Xanthe approached the door. She pushed down the handle. The lock disengaged. She shoved the door. It swung inwards.

Xanthe, Allissa and Leo stepped forwards and then froze in their tracks. A high-pitched wail streamed through the building.

71

Esin, her arms folded tightly, tapped an erratic patten with her fingertips. The lift struggled its way towards the basement, finally clunking into position. The doors strained open.

"Be ready," Esin hissed at Burak.

Burak removed the gun from its holster and levelled it at the empty carpark.

Esin indicated that they should wait. Long, silent seconds passed.

"It looks clear," Esin hissed. "Be careful."

Burak led the way out into the carpark, sweeping the gun one way and then the other.

Esin listened closely. Water dripped against the concrete. If anyone was watching them from the ill-lit recesses of the carpark, they were doing so in complete silence. The thought sent a shiver up Esin's spine.

They moved through the shadows and reached the vehicles in the far corner. Burak darted around a black BMW X5. He pulled the key from his pocket and unlocked the car. A high-pitched beep echoed through the carpark.

Fasslane pulled open one of the rear doors and shuffled inside. Esin slid into the passenger seat. Burak looked around the carpark one more time and then climbed into the driver's seat.

The BMW's engine roared and the lights blazed. Burak clicked the vehicle into reverse and pulled out of the bay. The strong headlights sliced through the night, illuminating the empty carpark. A modern looking Toyota sat against the wall at the far side. Esin considered stopping and somehow sabotaging the vehicle, but what would be the point. With Ramiz dead, the detectives had no idea where they were going. From here, the trail would go cold.

Burak swung the BMW in the direction of the exit. They barrelled up the ramp and into the evening. Esin glanced out of the window and up at the Sadik-Tech building. From here on out things were going smoothly, she could tell. A smile spread across her face.

72

At first Leo thought the high-pitched wail had come from Xanthe. Then he saw what she was looking at.

Three torch beams converged on an object in the middle of the room. It took Leo a few moments to work out what it was. Tied to a chair, but thrown backwards, Ramiz lay on the floor.

The young man screamed at the top of his lungs. The sound pounded against Leo's ear drums.

Xanthe charged forwards, speaking to Ramiz in a language Leo didn't understand. Ramiz turned and looking up at them with wide eyes. The screaming stopped.

"Help me with this," Xanthe said, struggling to lift the chair upright again.

"I'm so sorry," Ramiz sobbed. "That man said that if he saw me again, he would kill me. He almost shot me before." Leo noticed a bullet hole in the wall behind Ramiz. "I thought that was him coming back. I thought that was it."

Leo helped Xanthe right the chair and then stepped over to examine the bullet hole in the wall behind Ramiz.

Xanthe slid a knife from beneath her tunic and cut the bindings. Ramiz winched in pain.

"Are you hurt?" Allissa asked, sweeping the light of her torch across his body.

Ramiz shook his head.

Leo and Allissa exchanged a glance.

Ramiz rubbed as his wrists and slumped further into the chair. "They have Fasslane," he said, struggling to his feet. He took an unsteady step forward and hugged Xanthe. "They're planning to escape tonight. They've got an exit strategy planned for him. A place somewhere in the east where he'll lie low for a few months until this all blows over."

"That's great," Allissa said.

Through the window, the city glittered in the hazy night. In the distance the thick dark smudge of the Bosphorus loomed, spanned by the Fatih Sultan Mehmet Bridge.

"We can just tell everyone what you know, and blow this thing wide open," Allissa said.

"No, that won't work," Ramiz said. "That will just add fuel to the fire. We need proof. Proper, irrefutable evidence."

Leo nodded. "But what?"

Ramiz stared at something through the window. He didn't reply.

"Ramiz?" Allissa said. "What do we do? We need to stop them and expose Fasslane for the liar he is."

"There it is!" Ramiz shouted, pointing downwards.

They all rushed towards the glass. Seven floors below, an unassuming SUV slid out of the carpark. It paused for a moment at the intersection and then turned right.

Without answering, Ramiz spun around to face his sister.

Leo realised how alike they looked. Not just their slim figures and large eyes, but the way they moved.

"Did you bring my computer?" Ramiz asked.

"Yes of course, it's in the car," Xanthe replied.

"Excellent," Ramiz said, spinning to face Leo and Allissa. "Then we go after them ourselves."

"We don't know where they're going?" Leo said.

Ramiz and Xanthe set off across the office.

Leo turned back to look at Allissa, silhouetted against the city. She shrugged and ran after Ramiz and Xanthe, leaving Leo with an undisturbed view of the lights below. Leo sighed, then turned and gave chase.

73

Xanthe unlocked the car as they approached and then leapt into the driver's seat. Ramiz slid into the passenger seat beside her.

"Under the seat," Xanthe said, before Ramiz could even ask.

Ramiz bent over and pulled out a laptop. He cracked it open on his knees and fired it up.

Leo and Allissa scrambled into the back seats.

Xanthe started the car. It hummed gently as the electric motors warmed up.

"Where are we going?" She turned to her brother.

"One moment," Ramiz said, his fingers flying over the keyboard. "I'm just getting the details of the vehicle they used."

Leo peered around the chair and saw that Ramiz was scrolling through footage from the building's security cameras.

"I suppose you've used some cutting-edge tech to hack through their defences and get that?" he said.

Allissa rolled her eyes.

Ramiz glanced up at him. "No, I just logged in. They haven't changed the password since our dad died. It's actually his date of birth," Ramiz said, deadpan. "This next part is a bit trickier though, and slightly more illegal. They're in a BMW X5. There's no record of it on the company system, unless... ahhh! There we are!" He pointed at the screen and bounced up and down in excitement.

Xanthe tapped impatiently on the steering wheel.

"It's leased from a company in Başakşehir, and, wait a minute... yes, they do! Yes, they do!"

"He's always like this," Xanthe said, turning and shrugging apologetically at Leo and Allissa. "It'll make sense in a minute, when the rest of the world catches up."

Ramiz thrashed at the keyboard again. A map of Istanbul materialised, and a few moments later a pulsing blue dot appeared.

"There they are," Ramiz said, triumphantly pointing at the screen. "Turn left."

"How did you —" Leo started.

"It's best not to —" Xanthe interrupted, clicking the car into drive, and accelerating aggressively towards the exit ramp.

"Lease companies often install trackers in their vehicles in case of theft. Sure, BMWs have their own system which you can piggyback, but their encryption is like, you know, sigma grade stuff. The lease companies..."

Leo caught Allissa's eye. She grinned. Leo made a mental note not to ask Ramiz about technical things again.

"What now?" Xanthe asked as they sped north.

"They're heading towards the Asian side. They've just joined the E80 heading east. It's always been their plan to get Fasslane away from here. In no time they'll be out in rural Turkey, they'll switch cars and then we will never find them again."

Leo sunk back into the seat and thought hard. In every case so far, they had found some way to get ahead. They'd realised something or noticed something that made the whole thing make sense. It was about trying to understand the person on the other side, to get inside their thoughts and feelings.

Ramiz typed furiously, a look of anguish clouding his face.

"Hold on a minute," Leo said, sitting bolt upright. "What are they most afraid of?" His voice sounded loud in the silent car.

"What do you mean?" Xanthe asked, passing through an intersection without slowing down.

"If we know what they're afraid of most, we can try to understand their plan, or at least how to —"

"Fasslane being exposed as a liar," Ramiz said. "If there is clear, irrefutable evidence that Fasslane hasn't been taken by the Americans, or murdered by some secret society, then that disproves all of his claims. The business won't get its way with the ministry of defence and Fasslane will be seen as the idiot he actually is."

Allissa nodded. "But it would need to be in plain sight, for the whole world to see."

"There." Leo leaned forward and pointed at the map on the screen. "I think I've got a plan, and we need to do it right there."

As the brightly-lit curve of the E80 freeway came into view, Leo explained his plan. The others listened in raptured silence.

"I know just the people to help," Ramiz said when he'd finished, typing quickly.

74

Burak further depressed the accelerator of the BMW X5 as the illuminated towers of the Fatih Sultan Mamet Bridge rose into view. His thick knuckles gripped the steering wheel, and he scrutinised the traffic behind them for any sign that they were being followed. The road at this hour was almost empty. Perfect.

"Slow down," Esin hissed from the passenger seat. "We all want to get there as soon as possible, but we can't draw attention to ourselves. Especially with him —" she nodded towards Fasslane in the backseat, staring out the window. "Stay below 55."

"No one's following, boss. It's okay. We are alone," Burak replied, glancing in the mirror again. The distant headlights of other vehicles drifted around behind them, but nothing was close enough to be following.

"I don't care what you think you know," Esin snarled. "Getting there a few minutes sooner is not worth the risk. We're not ruining the plan now."

Burak glanced at the woman beside him. Her short bob-cut swung about her face as she turned to look out of the window. Dark trees flashed by on both sides of the road.

Burak took a deep breath and tried to relax. He removed his foot from the accelerator and the X5 slowed. He made a circular motion with his shoulders, trying to loosen the knot of tension which had taken up residence in the centre of his back. It didn't help.

"It's okay," Esin muttered quietly. "The plan is flawless. We will be in Uludağ in a couple of hours. Then we'll have good as disappeared."

Burak nodded, wanting to share his boss's confidence. All he could think about was the young man he'd left alive back at the office. Burak had stared into the large hazel-coloured eyes as his finger closed around the trigger. He'd levelled the gun at the young man's head and then…

Then nothing. The man hadn't screamed, shouted or begged. He sat motionless, simply waiting for something to happen.

Burak had killed countless men over the years, but right then, in the calm gaze of those hazel eyes, he couldn't do it. He hadn't wanted to do it.

Burak had raised a finger to his lips. Then, he'd fired a shot into the wall, kicked the chair backwards, and hurried from the office.

Driving the car, twenty minutes later, Burak hoped his moment of mercy wouldn't come back to bite him.

"You do not believe me?" Esin said, turning to face him. Her eyes bored into Burak's.

Burak nodded soberly, his eyes darting from the road ahead to the mirror.

They swept beneath the west tower of Fatih Sultan Mehmet bridge. The giant structure glowed purple against the blue-black night sky.

The X5 shot onto the bridge, the lights of Asian Istanbul dancing tantalisingly close across the surface of the water. A freighter glided beneath them, on route to the Red Sea.

Burak smiled, the scar on his left cheek distorting his expression into something of a sneer.

"You see," Esin said, patting him on the arm. "You had nothing to worry about. We'll be there soon, and then he can disappear." She pointed a thumb at Fasslane in the backseat. "Then there is nothing to incriminate us."

A strong set of headlights caught Burak's eye in the mirror. He glanced at it. Something was approaching them quickly in the right-hand lane.

Some idiot showing off on the empty night-time roads of the city, Burak thought.

The lights drew closer, dazzling Burak. He glanced at Esin in the seat beside him.

Esin turned and saw the vehicle approaching.

"It's nothing," she said, reading the worry in his face. "Let them pass. No problem." She shrugged.

Burak kept the X5 steady. The lights neared, splitting from two into six. Burak squinted in the mirror. If he wasn't mistaken, three large vehicles were gaining on them at over eighty.

The X5 passed the centre of the bridge. The thick cables that suspended the roadway flashed by in a stream of colour and then rose up again to meet the tower on the Asian side. The lights of the opposite bank, a blur of white and orange, were almost upon them.

Burak glanced into the mirror again. As the bright lights of the approaching vehicles closed in, colours danced across his vision. The shining sliver grill of the lead vehicle came into view. The rumble of their diesel engines rose above the sound of the X5.

Esin turned and squinted through the rear window. She shrugged and then settled back into her seat.

The approaching engines rose further, and then three large white trucks thronged past in the outside lane. The trucks swept into the glare of the X5's headlights. Burak recognised the logos emblazoned on the vehicles' sides.

Then, as though in military formation, the vehicles fanned out across the road before them. Driving side by side, they slowed, blocking the road ahead. A chain of brake lights lit up the road.

75

Xanthe's face locked into an expression of steely determination as she pushed the Toyota to its limit. Buildings flashed past on both sides. Lights streaked against the glass. Leo couldn't make out where they were going. He hoped silently that they wouldn't come across any police vehicles. Travelling at this speed was bound to attract attention.

Leo peered at Ramiz typing frantically on his laptop. It looked as though he was exchanging messages through an instant messenger system. Leo thought better of asking and settled back into the seat. A ball of tension knotted in his gut.

"We're five minutes from the bridge," Ramiz said, looking up from the screen. "Look, there!"

Leo recognised the tower of the Fatih Sultan Mehmet Bridge from their journey up the Bosphorus a few hours ago.

"Come on," Ramiz whispered, eyes flicking from the road to the screen and back again.

Xanthe accelerated past a heavily-loaded truck,

lumbering down the slow lane. Despite their speed, the Toyota remained quiet. Tyres rumbled against the road and the air conditioner hummed.

The road ahead straightened out. The bridge lay before them, dead ahead. Trees enclosed the road on both sides, flashing past in a blur.

Leo peered up at the tower as they neared. The Toyota powered past two cars. Then they were on the bridge.

Leo peered down at the oily black water beneath them. The bridge had looked so high when they slid beneath it just a few hours ago.

"Look! Look!" Ramiz shouted, his finger pointing through the windscreen. The brake lights of several vehicles flashed ahead. Although the road was quiet, a steady stream of traffic used the bridge, even in the middle of the night.

"Why is there a blockage at this time of night?" Leo asked.

Ramiz grinned.

Xanthe pulled into the fast lane and flashed the Toyota's lights. A pair of cars shuffled out the way.

Leo and Allissa strained upwards in their seats to see what was happening further down the road. To their right and left the lights of Istanbul twinkled hypnotically on the surface of the water, totally ignored by those in the car.

"Look at that!" Ramiz shouted, laughing out loud. He pointed at the laptop.

Leo leaned around the seat. The laptop showed a live news feed. A cameraman ran towards a stationary vehicle in the centre of the multi-carriageway road. Leo recognised the steel cables of the bridge.

"There they are!" Xanthe said, swerving around another car. Two more cars blocked their way now. Xanthe slammed on the brakes. The Toyota squealed to a stop.

Xanthe and Ramiz piled out of the Toyota, quickly followed by Leo and Allissa. They charged past several cars already caught up in the blockage. Numerous drivers protested on their horns. Wind whipped across the carriageway, almost pushing Leo into one of the waiting vehicles. Another impatient driver sounded the horn, the noise carried away by the strong cross-wind.

Leo reached the front of the waiting car and froze. Before them, in the middle of the carriageway, three news trucks totally blocked the bridge. And stopped before them, illuminated by floodlights attached to the news trucks and the headlights of the waiting cars, idled a BMW X5.

76

Inside the BMW, Esin fumed. She looked from the approaching cameramen, to Burak, and then at Fasslane in the back.

She tried to swallow, but something felt as though it was stuck in her throat.

"What shall we do, boss?" Burak said. All the colour drained from his face. His hands remained clamped to the steering wheel.

One of the cameramen approached Esin's window. The light attached to the camera shone into the car, washing everything in a ghostly glow. Esin covered her face in her hands — she still had a reputation to uphold and couldn't have them recognising her.

Through the window, Esin couldn't make out his words, but she could guess. She resisted the temptation to roll down the glass and knock the camera from his grasp.

Clearly not getting the shot he wanted, the cameraman moved to the back of the X5. A bolt of excitement shot through him as he recognised Fasslane through the darkened windows.

Esin swore under her breath.

"Boss?" Burak said, looking around. "We're completely blocked in here."

Esin peeked through her fingers and out in the direction of the city centre.

Two hundred feet below the roadway, the lights of a small boat bobbed and twinkled on the vast expanse of the Bosphorus. Then she looked at Burak beside her, his bulky frame wedged into the driving seat, his scarred face set into a grimace.

As though out of the Bosphorus itself, a plan began to form. Sure, this wasn't what they intended to happen, but the full story wasn't out yet. Maybe what they wanted was still achievable.

Headlines scrolled through Esin's mind. Quickly, in whispered Turkish, she explained her plan to Burak.

77

Leo watched, rooted to the spot, as cameramen encircled the BMW X5. Bright lights from the waiting cars illuminated the scene. Car horns and irked shouts carried down the roadway as more vehicles joined the delay. The night wind whipped and sung through the bridge's suspension cables. Far below, the distant waters of the Bosphorus lapped unseen. The lights of the far-off downtown cast an orange glow up into the sky.

Leo examined the news trucks for the first time. The logos of their networks shone on the gleaming white sides. Satellite dishes projected from the roofs. They were broadcasting the scene to the world. Live.

Ramiz stood between Leo and Allissa, his eyes wide, his body poised.

"How did —" Allissa pointed vaguely in the direction of the trucks.

"I've got a few trusted contacts in the industry," Ramiz said. "I help them find the truth on stories, or give them leads. This will make their careers."

One of the cameramen glanced at Ramiz and nodded

almost imperceptibly. The cameraman then wheeled around to get a shot of the waiting traffic. The lens swept past Leo and Allissa. Leo resisted the temptation to duck out of shot.

At that moment, the driver's door of the X5 swung open and a burly man leapt out.

"Burak," Allissa whispered, recognising the cropped hair and the scar which ran down the man's cheek.

This time he wore non-descript black clothes, his muscles rippling beneath.

Leo's feet froze in position. Visions of the last time they'd seen the man scrolled through his memory. Burak had already tried to kill them in the cistern and set them up at the airport. The man was not good news.

The camera operators turned to get Burak in the centre of their shots. They moved with fearless efficiency, as though for them this was just another day.

Burak yanked open the back door of the X5 and reached inside.

Leo held his breath.

The muscles in Burak's arms strained as he attempted to pull something sizable from the backseat. His feet slipped across the roadway, before finding grip. His mouth twisted into a grim scowl of determination. Burak pulled forward, and then the thing inside dragged him back. For long seconds the man strained and huffed, then finally he hauled his quarry clean out of the vehicle.

Another man sprawled down to the roadway. For a heartbeat he lay still, before his hands scrabbled against the tarmac in an attempt to crawl away.

Unaware of the audience, Burak slammed the rear door of the X5, then turned calmly to face the other man. The other man crawled impotently across the roadway, then attempted to struggle to his feet.

"Brent Fasslane," Allissa whispered. "It's got to be Fasslane."

"But, what is he —" Leo muttered.

Burak strode over to the man and lifted him effortlessly from the ground. In the lights of the waiting cars, Leo saw that Allissa was right. His hair was longer than before and stubble scudded around his face. He also wore the dark patches of someone with not enough sleep and too much worry. But the close together eyes, the short, rotund frame, the sandy hair — it was him. Sure as he'd ever been, Leo recognised the man as Brent Fasslane.

Burak twisted Fasslane's arm to breaking point. Fasslane howled and bobbed up and down. Burak, his biceps bulging and his chin jutting forward, forced Fasslane up onto his tip toes. Fasslane shrieked, the momentary outburst carried away on the howling wind.

Burak then turned away from the camera and shoved Fasslane across the roadway. Fasslane sprawled to the concrete a few feet away. Burak was on the man again in an instant, he lifted him up again and this time, half carried, half dragged him to the edge of the road.

Burak's intention occurred to Leo like a punch to the gut. At the same moment, realisation dawned on Fasslane. He fought and kicked more aggressively than before.

Burak reached the railing that ran down the side of the bridge. Two sets of railings separated the traffic from the void, and two hundred feet below that, the open water of the Bosphorus beckoned.

A hammer struck against Leo's heart. He wished his legs into action. Like an orchestra's crescendo, the timpani of his pulse rose in his ears.

Wind sung through the cables now.

Burak shoved Fasslane over the first set of railings. The smaller man fell headfirst to the concrete on the other side. The men were out of the glare of the waiting cars now.

The camera operators moved in silently, adjusting the lights mounted on top of their cameras.

Burak scrambled over the railing. Then, muscles rippling, he looked down at the smaller man. Fasslane scraped and clawed at the concrete, pulling himself a couple of feet away before Burak leaned over, grabbed him by the ankle, and pulled him back again.

Then, as if Fasslane weighed nothing, Burak lifted him clean from the concrete and shoved him up against the railing.

78

As though shaken from a trance, Leo, Allissa and Ramiz rushed forward. Leo and Ramiz ran directly at Burak, his imposing figure standing tall against the black water.

Burak held Fasslane in both hands, his arms extended. Fasslane kicked and struggled, even striking Burak on a couple of occasions. Burak weathered the impact without so much as a grimace. Fasslane gurgled unintelligibly, his eyes wide with fear. His fingers scratched at Burak's arms.

Leo and Ramiz scrambled over the inner railing and onto the narrow strip of concrete between the barriers. Leo gripped the outer fence, which came to just above his waist, and peered over. He shuddered. It was like looking into an abyss. Nothing was distinguishable below.

They ran up to Burak and attempted to pull Fasslane back from the edge. Leo seized the big man around the arms and yanked him back towards the roadway. Ramiz looped his hands around Fasslane's waist and pulled.

Burak grimaced, his scarred grin widening, but no one moved. Burak's strong feet remained rooted to the spot. His thick arms held Fasslane in a vice.

Leo leapt up and seized Burak around the neck. Tendons and veins bulged beneath Burak's waxy skin. To Leo, it felt like clutching a tree trunk. Using all the strength he had, Leo attempted to topple the man back towards the road and away from the perilous drop.

The wind howled harder now. Leo's hair covered his face. Gusts thundered past his ears, rendering him unable to hear.

A moment later the gusts subsided, and Leo heard a raised voice.

"Push!"

He recognized the voice. It was Allissa.

Leo glanced back towards the waiting cars. Allissa stood beside them, her face inches from Leo's ear.

"Trust me," Allissa said. "It's the only way. We push together."

Leo glanced at Ramiz. Both then turned to face Allissa and nodded in unison.

Together, all three of them stopped pulling Burak and Fasslane back towards the road and pushed them towards the void.

A momentary flicker of confusion lit Burak's face. Bracing himself against pressure from one direction, he was unprepared for the change. His feet shuffled to correct his movement a moment too late.

Leo, Allissa and Ramiz shoved harder. The steel railing banged against Burak's hip. They shoved again. The top-heavy man bent outwards over the void. In a state of panic, he let go of Fasslane, who crumpled, wheezing and panting to the floor.

The three shoved again, harder this time. Burak reached out, but seized only air. His arms flailed uselessly.

They pushed one more time. Thrashing the air, a cry parting his lips, Burak fell backwards into the void.

79

Esin clamped her hands across her face. She was determined that the news cameras wouldn't reveal her identity. She slid down in the seat and listened closely to the sound of movement and raised voices outside.

She counted the passing of another few seconds and then peeked through her fingers. At first, she saw the road ahead and the stationary news trucks in the small gap between her fingers. She twisted her head left and right, looking for the unwelcome, all-seeing lenses of the TV crews. Nothing. No one stood in front of the car. Twenty yards away, the TV trucks still blocked the road, but they appeared to be unmanned.

Esin lowered her hands and looked towards the edge of the bridge. She couldn't make out the action but could see that it had the attention of the surrounding cameras. Everyone was oblivious to her. Esin adjusted the X5's mirror and scanned the scene behind her. Several motorists had climbed from their cars and were watching enraptured.

Then, in the mirror, she saw the distant blue flicker of emergency vehicles. Police, probably. It would take them some time to get there through the backed-up traffic, but they would get here eventually. Time was not on her side.

Esin glanced to the left. Cars on the opposite side of the carriageway, heading back to European Istanbul, crawled past. She saw one woman slow to a walking pace, desperate to see what disaster had caused such a delay.

"Sick," Esin muttered, grinning to herself.

She snapped open the glovebox. A light twitched. She searched through the contents, pulling things out onto the floor. The car's rental documents, a packet of mints, an empty box of cigarettes, a wad of fuel receipts. Her fingers touched something hard and cold at the back of the compartment.

"There you are," she said, sliding the gun beneath her belt.

Then, slowly and quietly, she popped open the door and stepped out onto the tarmac.

80

"What have we done?" Leo shouted, rushing forwards and peering into the void. They'd just pushed a man from the bridge to certain death. Wind roared past his ears. The distant and indistinguishable waters lapped two hundred feet below. Leo couldn't believe what they'd done.

Allissa and Ramiz joined him at the railing. All three studied the scene for several moments. Then, their expressions of worry merged into beaming smiles.

Twenty feet below, barely visible beyond the glare of the lights, Burak struggled and fought on the end of a cable. He hung upside down, swinging from side to side.

Leo followed the cable with his eyes. Tied to one of Burak's ankles, it looped up and over the railing and then around one of the bridge's suspension cables.

Burak's voice drifted up to them as he struggled to right himself.

Leo shook his head slowly and then looked at Allissa. "How did you... how did you think to do that?"

"It was pretty simple really," Ramiz said, interrupting, his hands outstretched in explanation. "It's very clever. A simple balance of physical forces, calculations of weight, time, speed and density. Burak was clearly the heaviest, so trying to beat him on strength alone would be almost impossible, so I just —"

"Where's Xanthe?" Leo and Allissa interrupted in unison.

81

Two minutes earlier, as Ramiz, Allissa and Leo charged after Burak and Fasslane, Xanthe paused. Something told her to wait.

She looked around, all eyes, including the camera crews, were focused on the brawling men. To Xanthe that all seemed a little too convenient. She didn't know for certain, but it would be unlike Esin Kartan to miss an event like this.

Xanthe stepped behind one of the stationary cars. The driver stood beside his car, straining to see the action.

Xanthe crouched in behind the car's front wing. She peered out over the bonnet and surveyed the scene.

A flurry of shouts echoed from the far side of the bridge as Burak and Fasslane continued to brawl.

Xanthe stayed focused, scanning the TV trucks and the BMW.

A faint click drifted from the BMW. Xanthe dropped out of sight and peered beneath the car.

Slowly and silently, a pair of shoes stepped down from the door.

Another flurry of shouts echoed from the fighting men.

Xanthe ignored it. Her eyes locked on the shoes as they took a tentative step towards the rear of the BMW. The door clicked softly closed.

Xanthe stood up slowly and tried to peer through the BMW. The blacked-out glass made it impossible to see anything on the other side. She crouched down again and watched Esin run towards the road's central barrier.

Xanthe leapt to her feet and pounded across the tarmac. She swung around the rear of the large car.

Esin stood six feet away, looking into the oncoming traffic.

Thoughts of her father's death swarmed Xanthe's mind. Her muscles tensed, ready for conflict. She lunged forward, her shoes slipping across the gritty tarmac, and looped her arm around Esin's neck, pulling her backwards. Xanthe had expected Esin to sprawl to the floor, where she could be restrained until help arrived. Esin didn't move. Xanthe pulled as hard as she could.

Esin's muscles tensed into coils of steel beneath her skin.

Esin glanced over her shoulder and caught Xanthe's eye. Xanthe recognised something like a sneer. Her stomach lurched. She attempted to pull the woman off balance again. Nothing happened.

Esin steadied herself, her strong legs finding grip on the roadway. She bent her knees and dipped into a crouch. She raised her hands and gripped on to Xanthe's forearms.

Xanthe felt a vice closing across her skin. The wailing sirens faded into a muted cry against her pounding heart. She glanced behind her, in the hope that someone was heading to her aid, but they were hidden by the parked BMW.

Esin heaved, grunted, and swung Xanthe into the air.

Xanthe spun upside down. Her arms flailed, clawing

only air. She landed hard onto the road. The breath lurched from her lungs. She looked around in a daze.

Traffic roared. A car horn howled. Xanthe realised all at once that Esin had thrown her into the path of oncoming traffic.

She rolled to the edge of the road. A horn shrieked. Tyres thundered past inches from her face, spraying dust and gravel into her eyes and mouth.

Xanthe spun onto her back and scrambled to her feet.

Esin leapt across the central reservation in one swift movement. Fire burned in the older woman's eyes.

Xanthe spat gravel from her mouth, then charged forwards. She aimed two punches at Esin's chest. Esin ducked them easily and then flung a kick at Xanthe's ribs. Esin was fast and powerful. Xanthe attempted to spin out of the way, but only managed to lessen the impact. A searing pain shot through her abdomen.

Xanthe took a step backwards.

The roadway shook beneath the wheels of a truck.

Xanthe took another step back and glanced around. For a moment the strong cross-wind subsided, revealing the scream of nearby sirens. Xanthe glanced over her shoulder. Strobing blue lights picked their way through the blocked-up traffic behind them. They would be here in a couple of minutes.

"It's over," Xanthe shouted, putting her palms out. "There's no point fighting. The police will be here soon."

Esin snarled and glanced from the approaching blue lights to the road behind her, and then on to Xanthe. She retained her fighting stance.

Xanthe took another step backwards, buying time.

Esin glanced behind her again. A car rumbled towards

them in the middle lane, its headlights piercing through the night.

Esin swung back towards Xanthe. She shook her head. "Oh no, I don't think it's over quite yet," she said.

In one swift movement, Esin pulled a gun from beneath her clothes and strode towards Xanthe.

Xanthe tried to swallow, tried to breathe. It felt like her feet were set into the concrete of the bridge itself.

The approaching sirens faded into the distant hubbub.

Esin grabbed her, pressing the gun into her stomach, and then forced them both into the path of the oncoming car.

82

Leo, Allissa and Ramiz searched the scene before them for signs of Xanthe. To their right, the TV trucks still sat blocking the traffic. To the left, cars waited for the blockage to pass, many motorists standing beside their vehicles. Several police cars now picked their way slowly through the congestion.

The X5 sat motionless, behind which the occasional car streamed towards the European side of the city. Then a car, its tyres screeching over the asphalt, sped in the opposite direction.

Allissa, Leo and Ramiz dashed forward, swerved around the X5 and peered over the central reservation. In the distance a small yellow car powered down the inside lane.

"Xanthe," Ramiz said, breathless. "She must have been taken by... Esin."

"She had an escape already planned out," Leo said, watching the taillights shrink to specks in the night. "She just didn't expect us to stop her here."

Allissa nodded and then looked at Ramiz. Shock etched its way on to the man's thin face. "Did she give you any indication of what they had planned?" Allissa asked. "You said she was boasting about everything."

Ramiz shook his head. "Nothing. She just said they would be out of the city, and no one would find them, or something like that."

"Can't we just trace the car?" Leo pointed at the ghostly shape which was now almost invisible.

"How?" Ramiz said.

"You know, triangulate the immobiliser from something." Leo shrugged.

"No." Ramiz shook his head seriously. "We don't even know what car that is."

"Hack the traffic cameras?" Allissa said hopefully.

"That'll take too long." Ramiz looked down at his feet. His shoulders folded and he shrunk in stature.

The whine of the sirens was almost upon them now. Leo turned to look at the approaching lights, shuffling through the blocked-up traffic. The voice of a police officer, berating a slow-moving motorist, carried through the air.

"I can help you."

Leo, Allissa and Ramiz were startled by an American voice. They turned towards the sound.

"I know where they're going," Fasslane said, breathlessly. No one had heard him approach. He wiped the bedraggled hair from his eyes. "Get me out of here before the cops arrive, and I'll show you."

83

"I don't know how you expect to get away with this. Now you're adding kidnapping to your list of charges." Xanthe glanced back at Esin who sat behind her in the back of the bright yellow Renault Clio. The young woman in the driving seat sobbed as she powered them towards a the ramp.

"Shut up," Esin bellowed, the gun wavering between Xanthe and the driver. "Keep going, faster!"

Fortunately, they had only passed two other cars. Both had flashed their lights and slowed as they passed.

They powered off the motorway and turned left at a roundabout.

"Stop there. Stop there!" Esin shouted, pointing at a bus stop at the side of the road.

The distressed young woman slid the car to a stop.

"Now get out," Esin shouted.

The young woman leapt out of the vehicle.

"I'm sure the police will be along soon," Xanthe said. "Don't worry."

"You," Esin barked at Xanthe. "Drive."

Xanthe scrambled over the central console and into the

driver's seat. She readjusted the mirror and then pulled away, following Esin's instructing to rejoin the E80 highway on the correct side.

Watching the young woman whose car they'd stolen grow small in the mirror, Xanthe hoped she was right about the police arriving soon. Otherwise, they would be long gone.

84

"We need you to get this truck moved, now!" Ramiz shouted at one of the camera operators.

Recognising Ramiz as the original source of their tip off, the man shouted at his colleague inside the truck. A few moments later, the engine coughed into life and the truck rolled forward.

Ramiz leapt into the X5 alongside Allissa in the driver's seat. Leo and Fasslane climbed into the back.

Allissa touched the accelerator and the car's auto-start engaged. The key had never been removed from the ignition. She clicked the automatic gearbox into drive. They shot past the trucks and away from the flickering lights of the police. Allissa hammered the engine, the needles flickering up into the red, as the towers of the bridge faded into the night sky.

Allissa took the next exit and then pulled into a side street. The shadows hung thick around drooping trees. Several cats scurried across the narrow street and out of sight between two buildings.

Allissa killed the engine. The X5 grumbled into silence. She turned to face Fasslane in the back.

Fasslane stared morosely at his hands.

"We've got you away from the police, for now," Allissa said.

Fasslane glanced up at her and then back down at his fingers.

Allissa wondered how the confident and charismatic man she'd seen on the video had turned into such a wreck.

"Now you need to start talking," Leo demanded.

Fasslane looked up at Allissa and then at Leo. His lips moved as though he were about to speak, but the words never came out.

"We haven't got all night. You talk now, or I'll drive you straight back to the police on the bridge," Allissa said, her voice hard.

Fasslane nodded, his lips twitching. "Esin has a place. She called it the cabin. It's in Uludağ."

In the passenger seat, Ramiz paled.

"She said that no one knows about the place. It's off the record. Bought in a fake name or something, many years ago. She's got a car there that's clean too. We were going to go there for a night, maybe two. Then I would take the clean car further east. She had it all planned out."

"How far is that?" Leo asked. Allissa turned and poked at the sat nav in the dashboard.

"It's about 200km. We could be there in around three hours. Maybe nearer two if we don't hang around."

Ramiz pointed at Fasslane. "Uludağ." A cloud of concern moved across his face.

Fasslane nodded.

"Do you know it?" Allissa turned to face Ramiz.

"No. Well, maybe." Ramiz looked at Allissa in wide-eyed shock. "I've only been there once. It was ten years ago. To see the place my father was killed in the car wreck."

85

The silence in the Renault Clio was only broken by Esin barking directions to Xanthe. As the car purred down the D575 motorway, Xanthe tried to figure out their destination. They were generally heading south. Maybe they were heading for Izmir, Usak or on to Antalya itself. She had no clue.

Xanthe glanced at Esin in the passenger seat, the gun cradled in her lap. Xanthe wondered whether Esin would lose her focus at any moment, giving Xanthe the opportunity to try something.

As though reading her mind, Esin stared closely at Xanthe. She switched the gun from her right to her left hand.

Some time later they passed through the town of Bursa. Xanthe looked around at the squat concrete buildings. Most lay in darkness, the residents still hours away from rising. A few twinkled with the lights of early activity.

In the distance, against the star-studded sky, Xanthe recognised the brooding figure of Uludağ. The mountain soared above the town, as though threatening to blot out the sky altogether. A chime of something akin to realisation appeared in her mind. She focused in on it, tried to make sense of it. As yet it wouldn't come.

Xanthe played with the thought, as Esin navigated them out of the town and onto a mountain road.

Thick foliage surrounded them on both sides. The little car whined and struggled up the incline. The road twisted skywards, frost now hanging on the trees. Through the occasional break in the trees, Xanthe saw the lights of Bursa growing small beneath them. With the altitude, the weather closed in too.

"It's funny, even after all these years, this road reminds me of your father," Esin said.

Xanthe glanced at her. The older woman toyed with the gun, smiling.

"You don't remember do you? Oh bless," Esin said.

Realisation pinned Xanthe to the seat, pushing her shoulders back into the padding.

"There we are," Esin said, watching Xanthe's expression turn to stone. "The moment of realisation can be a beautiful thing."

"Our father died on this road," Xanthe whispered, glancing from the road ahead to Esin.

"Correct," Esin said.

"You?" Xanthe hissed between gritted teeth.

Esin cackled, slapping her thigh with amusement. "I think your father overestimated his dear children. Imagine you two in charge of a billion-lira business! Ha!"

"Why?" Xanthe said in astonishment. "No wait, I know. You wanted the business when he retired, and he wouldn't give it to you."

"Correct again," Esin said, nodding.

At that moment, light and the thronging of a powerful engine filled the Renault. Xanthe glanced in the mirror. Two fingers of light swept up the road behind them.

86

ALLISSA DROVE QUICKLY down the empty streets. She had to admit, the X5 was a great vehicle to drive. It had the power to cruise at high speeds, without reducing comfort. It was the polar opposite to the rust bucket Leo had bought a few months ago.

On the entire two-and-a-half-hour journey, only a few words were spoken in the car. The four wore expressions of fatigue and anxiety.

Allissa powered out of the town of Bursa and on to the slender road leading up towards Uludağ. Trees flanked the road on both sides. Allissa glanced up at the mountain to their left. Snow covered the high flanks of the imposing slopes. She slid down the window, letting a cool breeze whip into the car. Below them, the lights of the town sparkled, signalling they had already climbed a few hundred feet.

Allissa powered the X5 around a sharp corner. The thick tyres slid for a moment, sending a cloud of dust and gravel pinging into the barrier. Allissa applied the brake gently and slowed the car. Losing control on a road like this could be fatal.

The X5 rounded the corner, revealing a curve of tarmac leading up and around the mountain slope.

"There, look!" Ramiz shouted from the passenger seat. The small man shot up, suddenly alert. He sat forward in his seat; his finger pointed through the windscreen.

"What?" Allissa said, scanning the road ahead of them. Concentrating on getting them around the perilous corner, she had missed whatever he'd seen.

Leo and Fasslane leaned upwards from the back seats.

"There was a car. I'm sure of it." Ramiz shook his finger frantically. "The rear lights. It just went around the next corner."

Allissa peered up into the night but saw nothing. She clicked the car into manual transmission, gripped the wheel, and depressed the accelerator. The X5 leapt forward, the engine barely purring. Approaching the corner, she dropped down a gear and goaded the engine onwards. The rev counter strobed into the red, but the car stayed on course.

They swung around the corner, tyres screeching and dust flying into the air. The next curve of the mountain road appeared ahead of them, lying silver in the moonlight.

"There. There!" Ramiz shouted, bouncing in the seat.

Sure enough, three hundred feet ahead, a small yellow car climbed the mountain road.

"That's them, I'm sure of it!" Ramiz said.

"How sure?" Allissa glanced at him. "We only saw them at a distance."

"Sure. Totally sure."

The X5 powered on, Allissa moving through the gears. The other car disappeared around another corner. Allissa steeled her expression and pushed them on. When the car appeared again, it was just sixty feet ahead. The road stretched out for at least half a mile now.

"Okay, now we'll find out." Allissa hammered the accelerator. The X5 grunted and then rocketed forwards. Allissa gripped the wheel, steering them into the oncoming lane. Within a few seconds they were pulling alongside the yellow car.

Allissa peered into the car. Sure enough, Xanthe and Esin looked back at her. Xanthe wore an expression of fear. Esin snarled.

Allissa's eyes flicked back to the road ahead. The next corner was approaching fast. Her foot hovered over the accelerator for a moment, then she saw the lights of another vehicle approaching. She hit the brake, sending them all jarring into their seat belts. She swung the wheel and pulled them into the lane behind the yellow car. An old Land Rover rumbled around the corner, passing them by inches.

"We've got to stop them," Fasslane said, his voice weak. "If Esin gets to her cabin with the new vehicle, she'll be untraceable."

Allissa thumped the accelerator again. The X5 gained on the small car easily. Allissa pulled out again into the other lane. She was just about to overtake when the yellow car broke heavily. Red lights filled the BMW. Allissa squinted and stamped on the brake.

An almighty crunch vibrated through the BMW, followed by the sound of shattering glass.

Then, the driver's door of the Renault shot open.

87

"Faster, we have to lose them," Esin snarled. "We're almost there."

Xanthe squinted in the headlights. The powerful car was gaining on them again, trying to force them off the road.

The X5 attempted to overtake. Xanthe let the Renault slow, giving them a chance.

"Faster, I told you!" Esin jabbed her in the ribs with the gun. "I'm not afraid to use this. You're no good to me if you're not going to drive properly."

Xanthe reluctantly increased their speed. Headlights cut through the night ahead and their pursuers swerved back into lane behind them.

Xanthe glanced at Esin. The older woman turned around in the passenger seat and watched the approaching vehicle. The gun hung loose in her grasp.

Xanthe seized her chance. She hit the brake as hard as she could. For a moment the Renault slid, tyres roaring across ice and gravel. Then they found grip and the Renault screamed to a stop.

Esin careered into the dashboard. Light filled the small car, followed by the sound of shattering glass.

The breath lurched from Xanthe's lungs. Her ears screamed.

Xanthe spun around in the seat and slapped the gun from Esin's grasp. It thudded to the floor somewhere in the rear footwell.

Esin made a grab for Xanthe, her fingers outstretched like that of a giant cat. Xanthe moved backwards a moment too late. A sharp, hot pain lashed through her face.

Xanthe struck Esin with an elbow and then a blow to the stomach. Before the woman could recover, she undid her seatbelt and threw open the driver's door.

Esin screamed and made a grab for Xanthe's arm. Xanthe lashed out again, knocking her sideways. Before Esin could take another swing, Xanthe leapt from the car and ran towards the BMW.

88

Allissa hit the brakes hard and swung the wheel to the right. The BMW's left wing smashed into the back of the smaller car. Glass shattered and metal groaned. One of the headlights went out. The seatbelt cut hard against Allissa's chest.

She pushed herself back into the seat and forced herself to breathe. She peered out at the smaller car and then around at the other passengers. The sound of the crash rung loud in her ears.

Allissa snapped the X5 into reverse and pulled away. The two cars creaked as their twisted skins disentangled.

Leo and Ramiz pushed open their doors and scrambled out.

The single working light of the BMW cast a strange angular light through the scene. Shadows and reflections bounced from the splintered rear of the Renault.

Leo picked his way towards the Renault, ready to jump or run at a moment's notice.

The engine of the X5 growled gently. Leo's body shook

with the cold. His light clothes were no match for the mountain temperatures.

The Renault rocked twice and then the door flew open.

Leo and Ramiz took a step further forward.

Xanthe appeared from the driver's door of the little car. She ran towards Ramiz, fear etched into her expression.

Ramiz briefly embraced his sister. Leo strode towards the driver's door.

"Esin has a gun," Xanthe said, breathlessly pointing at the Renault.

Leo froze in his position. The Renault was just six feet away. Something moved in the shadows of the car's interior.

"Leo, be careful!" Xanthe shouted again.

The Renault's engine whined gently. Leo bent down and peered through the shattered rear windscreen. Something moved inside. In the strange half-light from the BMW's single headlight, he couldn't see Esin clearly.

"Step out of the car now," Leo shouted, forcing confidence into his voice. "The police will be here very soon," he lied.

The noise which came from the car sounded more animal than human.

Leo strode around to the open driver's door. He reached towards the ignition block, aiming for the keys which still dangled there.

The door slammed shut before he reached it. He glanced up and saw Esin in the driver's seat. The woman sneered at him and then revved the engine.

"Wait, wait!" Leo shouted, scrambling for the door handle.

The tyres spun, flinging dust, glass and shards of broken metal into the air.

Leo grabbed the handle just as the car pulled away, the front swinging violently up the road.

"Get in, now!" Allissa yelled, revving the larger and more powerful engine of the BMW.

Xanthe and Ramiz piled in the back, and Leo leapt into the passenger seat. The doors slammed and Allissa pulled away.

The Renault sped up the road ahead of them, cutting two deep and twisting tyre tracks into freshly laid snow. Allissa squinted at the single working taillight, just a pinprick of red against the moonlit night. Clearly Esin was pushing the car to the maximum.

Ahead, the road curved to the left. Leo watched closely, expecting to see a flicker from the Renault's brake lights. None came. Esin continued to accelerate away.

"The corner," Leo said, pointing. "She's going way too fast for the corner."

89

Esin pushed the pedal to the floor as the small car climbed the icy road. The wheels, which had spun and fishtailed to the right and left, had now found a steady forward motion.

Esin studied the road ahead. It was just a couple of miles to the cabin. Just a little closer and she could make it on foot. That way they wouldn't be able to follow her — or at least, they wouldn't know where she'd gone. Footsteps were impossible to follow through the thick woodland which stretched up the mountain slopes either side of the road.

They would be so close, but impossibly far too. If she could just get out of sight she would make a dash for it.

Esin glanced in the mirror. The BMW had started to pick its way up the slope behind her. Whilst it was a vastly more suitable vehicle, the driver didn't know where they were going. Esin had been driving these roads for decades. She knew every rise and fall, every twist and turn.

Approaching the corner, Esin squeezed harder on the accelerator. The engine's hum became a whine. Tyres grunted and sloshed through the snow, struggling for traction. The corner neared, but the small car still careered forwards.

Esin bit her lip as her frozen hands held the wheel hard left. Through the windscreen the steel crash barrier, protecting traffic from a perilous drop, loomed ever closer.

"Come on, come on," she whispered to herself.

The tyres groaned, kicking snow and dirt in great arcs either side of the car.

At some point the tyres would cut through the snow and find traction. The car wobbled to the left and then to the right.

The barrier drifted ever closer. The thin metal strip filled the windscreen, beyond which, the featureless night sky stretched out into nothing.

The car rumbled and shook. Then, by some miracle, the tyres hit solid ground. The Renault leapt forward, dirt and gravel spraying up all around.

The acceleration pinned Esin into her seat. The car swung wildly to the right and left. The headlights swept from the road ahead, out into the void, and back again. The car flew on, bouncing from one side of the road to the other.

Esin glanced in the mirror and then at the corner ahead. The BMW had yet to round the bend.

If she could just get to the next corner and up into the woods before they caught up with her, then she would be free. She straightened out the wheel and steeled her expression.

Then, as though in slow motion, the car slipped to the left.

90

Allissa nudged the BMW around the corner, resisting the urge to accelerate. Speed on roads like this, she knew, could be deadly.

The X5's single headlight cast a solitary beam out into the night sky, then swept across to the road in front of them. A gasp sounded throughout the car.

A hundred feet ahead, further up the mountain road, the Renault lost the control. Tyre marks crisscrossed the road. Snow and ice sprayed up in all directions.

The car spun twice, then slowed.

Five pairs of eyes watched it from the X5. Allissa carefully increased speed towards the stricken vehicle.

The Renault spun one more time, then rolled towards the edge of the mountain road. No barrier stood here. The road just gave way to a perilous drop. In the murk, far below, icy trees shivered.

Allissa increased their speed again. The BMW made quick progress on the frozen road.

The Renault's wheels locked as Esin tried to stop. The car continued to slide. Tyres rattled through compacted snow. The rear of the Renault slid clear of the precipice. Another gasp reverberated through the X5. All eyes locked on the small yellow car ahead.

The Renault slowed but continued to drift backwards. The rear wheels rolled clear of the abyss. The car dropped on to its chassis. A stream of rock and ice skipped down the mountain, disappearing amid the trees. The Renault rocked; an awful scraping noise echoed around the mountain.

Allissa pulled the X5 slowly to a stop ten feet from the Renault. The X5's single beam washed the scene in cool bright light. The Renault lay still, teetering on the edge. In the driver's seat, Esin gripped the wheel. She still wore a strange expression of determination.

Leo and Allissa leapt out of the BMW and ran towards the Renault. Ramiz, Xanthe and Fasslane followed.

Leo ran forwards and grabbed the Renault's front bumper. He heaved as hard as he could. The car wouldn't move. Allissa joined him. Nothing happened.

"Stop!" Esin shouted from the driver's seat.

"We'll get you out," Leo shouted back. Wind whipped around his ears. "Ramiz, Xanthe, search for a rope, or something we can use to —"

"No," Esin interrupted. "Leave me."

Leo heard the gearbox of the Renault click as Esin changed gear. Even that small movement caused the car to rock.

"No," Leo said. "We will get you out of there." Leo stood back and walked around the car. The driver's seat was still above solid ground, maybe they could somehow reach her before the car toppled.

"No," Esin yelled, returning both hands to the steering wheel.

The sound of the Renault's engine grew from an idle murmur to a whine.

"No! Stop!" Leo shouted, running back to the front of the car. He tried to grab the bumper again. Allissa seized his shoulder and pulled him away from the car.

Esin released the clutch and the front wheels spun, sending snow and grit flying towards the onlookers. The tyres found traction on the road's edge. The car groaned. Metal screamed against concrete. Then gravity took over. The engine noise died. The Renault slid backwards, grinding against the road's edge. Something scraped and cracked. The car slipped backwards.

Through the windscreen, Esin's face set into something of a smile.

The car slid freely for a few moments, before crashing into the mountain slope. Glass shattered and a tyre popped. The Renault rolled backwards, exposing its scarred underside. More glass shattered. The roof twisted and thumped against the savage rocks.

Leo and Allissa stepped towards the cliff edge. The car continued to bump and crash, further into the darkness.

Leo inhaled a lungful of mountain air and intertwined his fingers with Allissa's.

"We can't save everyone," he said against the whipping wind.

"Not everyone deserves saving," Allissa replied.

91

Dawn broke slowly across the slopes of Uludağ. First, the sky lightened to a deep purple, muting the swathes of stars to a bullish few. Then a stripe of angry red rose, taking a few more stars with it. Finally, sometime later, creamy sunlight streamed across the horizon, washing out the stars altogether.

Leo and Allissa stood at the railing of a cabin and looked out at the coming day. Leo put his arm around Allissa's waist and pulled her in close.

"It's a nice place," Leo said, looking up at the cabin. It was constructed from wood and tiles. Ice hung in long fingers from the eves.

"Yeah, it is. A perfect place to hide from evil crimes, right?" Allissa replied, looking up at Leo. The light of the breaking dawn reflected in her eyes.

"Maybe we should get a place like this, forget about the city altogether. What do you think?"

Allissa looked out to the horizon. "With the nearest shop over ten miles away? No chance. I've always preferred cities anyway. You know where you are with a city; they wear their heart on their sleeve. Out here, anyone could be doing anything."

Leo was about to argue, but then realised Allissa's bonkers logic made some sort of sense. He laughed, his breath escaping in a thick cloud.

Leo looked down at the X5 parked at the end of the track below them. It had taken them almost an hour, using Fasslane's scant directions to find the cabin.

"Something tells me you enjoyed driving that thing, though?" Leo pointed at the car.

"Yes, it's a nice car," Allissa said. Leo went to speak, and Allissa interrupted him. "Absolutely no to your next question."

"But —"

"Guys, I think we're ready," Xanthe said, appearing at the cabin's front door.

The inside of the cabin was warm and welcoming. A fire burned in the hearth, and cups of coffee steamed from the table.

"Esin thought of everything here," Xanthe said, handing Leo and Allissa each a cup. "There's enough food and fuel for a couple of weeks at least."

"Are you sure I have to do this?" Fasslane's anguished voice interrupted Xanthe.

Allissa, Xanthe and Leo turned to face him. Ramiz stood in the far corner holding a smartphone.

"You have two options," Allissa replied firmly. "You do this now, or you take your chances with the police. You've caused a lot of people a lot of trouble in the last few weeks."

"I do this and then I can disappear?" Fasslane said.

The four exchanged glances. Each knew that the real villain had already faced justice. Their quarrel wasn't with this man.

"Yes," Leo said. "We will leave you here. You can stay or go as you please."

Fasslane nodded and then looked down at his hands.

"Ready?" Ramiz said, checking the settings on the camera.

Fasslane nodded again.

Ramiz gave a thumbs up gesture.

Allissa and Leo glanced at each other and then took long sips of the coffee.

Fasslane looked into the camera and began to speak. "My name is Brent Fasslane. I'm recording this to tell you that the claims in my book, A New World Order, are untrue..."

92

Brighton. A week later.

Green strode into the front room of Leo and Allissa's flat. Boxes were piled against the wall of the room, overflowing with books, dvds, and other stuff ready for the move.

"I don't know how you did it," he said, pointing a finger first at Leo, then Allissa. "But you did it. Absolutely incredible. A video from the man himself confirming that it was all a figment of his imagination. Amazing. I thought you'd come up with some evidence, or something, not a bloody personal confession. Where is he now?"

"He's gone underground. And I don't expect we'll be seeing him for some time," Leo said, dropping a pair of travel guides into the least overflowing box.

"Well, that doesn't really matter, I suppose. But wow, just wow. I owe you big time for this. Fasslane's confession has been the most watched video on the planet. This is big. Giant even." Green's face glowed.

"You gave us the info," Allissa said, a smile lighting her face. "As usual, we just went down the rabbit hole."

"You did a fantastic job of it, I can tell you that. But I'm here to give you another opportunity, actually. This could make you some big money. I'm talking tens of thousands. All I'd need is an on-record interview with you about what you did and how it came together. A blow-by-blow kind of thing."

Leo and Allissa glanced at each other. "We could tell you," Leo said, walking to the front door and holding it open. "But you would never believe us."

"Okay, okay." Green held his hands out in front of him. "You name your fee. This is, quite literally, the biggest story in the world right now. Whatever you want, I can get it for you."

"See you later Marcus," Allissa said, dropping a stack of magazines into another box.

Green turned to face Leo. "You name the price. This would blow up."

"Bye now," Leo said, nodding towards the door.

Green shook his head slowly and stepped towards the door. On the threshold he turned back into the room. "You know what, there's always been something different about you two. I don't understand it, but I absolutely love it." He slid a hand into his jacket pocket and handed Leo a business card. "If you do change your mind, give me a call, anytime. Day or night." Then Marcus Green turned and disappeared down the narrow staircase.

Leo looked down at the card, a thought emerging in his mind.

93

Brighton. Another week later.

"I'm going to miss this place," Allissa said, clattering out through the doors of their local pub.

"We'll come back, I'm sure," Leo said, joining her on the pavement.

Leo pulled his coat tightly around himself. Allissa looped her scarf around her neck one more time. Autumn was on the turn into winter. Cold air pushed in from the sea.

"We're not going to come all the way out here from our new place, though, are we?" Allissa said.

"I don't think we'll ever have to leave, with our beautiful sea views and integrated appliances," Leo said, mimicking the voice of the agent who had showed them around.

"You bloody better," Allissa said, digging him in the ribs. "I'm not being one of those people who just stays in all the time. You'll miss it though too, right? You've been here longer than me."

They reached the corner, and the Victorian building

that contained their flat came into view. Their window on the top floor looked dark and forlorn. Leo stopped and stared up at the building. A cold wind whipped around the corner. Leo shuddered.

"There's something I need to tell you," Leo said.

"Can it wait until we get inside, it's cold." Allissa shivered dramatically.

"No," Leo said, rooted to the spot. "Can you see anything different?" Leo pointed up at their building.

Allissa sighed and turned to face the house.

"No, I don't think — let's just get —"

"Look closely." Leo put his arms around Allissa and pulled her in close.

"Wait, the for sale sign. It's gone!" Allissa spun around to face Leo. "What... I don't understand."

"Well, earlier today I made a phone call and, I, well, I've bought us the flat."

Allissa's jaw hung slack with astonishment. Her eyes locked on Leo's. She muttered some unintelligible words, then shook her head as though trying to loosen the thought. "You can't have done that," she said finally. She folded her arms. "I don't understand. We have nowhere near enough money even for the deposit."

Leo looked down at the pavement. "Yeah, well. I did the interview with Green. He paid enough for a generous down payment on the place, and the monthly payments are almost the same as we were paying anyway. Come on, let's get inside, it's freezing." Leo strode off towards the door.

Allissa snapped her jaw shut and followed. "Wait, wait, wait!" she said, charging into the hallway behind him. "What did you tell him?"

"Well, I might have made a few things up," Leo said,

climbing the stairs. "In fact, he sent me a copy of the article earlier. I'll let you read it. But more importantly" — Leo stopped on the top step and turned to face Allissa — "It's my pleasure to now say... welcome home."

AN EXCERPT FROM THE DAILY MESSENGER

We stopped the New World Order. An interview with Leo Keane, one of the investigators responsible for exposing the Brent Fasslane scandal.

By Marcus Green

"It was nothing, really," Leo says, grinning at me from across the table in a pub in his home city of Brighton. "You know, we were in the right place at the right time, that sort of thing."

I remind him that this was the same scandal that saw the relationships between several world-powers sour, protests in the streets, and embarrassed a lot of important people. He grins and takes another sip of his drink.

"You're right," he says, finally. "But it wasn't as difficult as you might think. We have been doing these sorts of things for a while now," he reminds me. He's right, of course. In the last two years, Leo, along with his partner Allissa, have become experts at this. Shooting to notoriety during the trial of Allissa's father, Blake Stockwell (64), they've found several missing people around the globe.

"The thing is," Leo says, "people think they can just move on to another place without leaving a trace, but that's not true. Wherever you go there are clues to your next intention and indications of where you've been. As investigators, we're finely tuned to notice things like this. Take this bar, for example. We're not bothering anyone here, but I bet at least ten people could vouch for us being here, as well as multiple cameras."

What Leo's really talking about is how they found Brent Fasslane, holed up in a mountain cabin, when the rest of the world had no idea where he was.

"The big break came for us in this case when we tracked down a maid who had been working at the hotel in Istanbul where Fasslane had stayed. It's amazing what people notice, if it's unusual. She'd been cleaning his room one day and noticed he had a lot of cold weather clothing in a suitcase." Leo explained how this led them to believe that his next move had been to somewhere cold. "All we had to do is look for nearby places where the temperatures are cooler at that time of year. Uludağ was our first thought. It's just a few hours away by car and doesn't cross any international borders. We travelled out there and spent an afternoon asking people if a lone American man had been staying on the mountain, and we got lucky. As I say, right place, right time."

I remind Leo of the reported incident on the Fatih Sultan Mehmet Bridge and the rumours that an underground group call the Guardians of Truth were involved.

"Now you're the one making things up, Marcus," he replies, smiling again. "Haven't you learned anything at all from Fasslane's book?"

Leo and Allissa next case will take them somewhere very close to home, to London...

GET LONDON NOW

Anna thought she had the perfect life, until she realised it wasn't hers to begin with.

When Anna's husband dies in a boating accident, she's heartbroken. Together, they had the perfect lives, and if the IVF went well, hopefully soon a family.

In an attempt to reconnect with her husband's estranged family, Anna heads to London. But, after a chance encounter with a familiar looking stranger, what she knew about the love of her life begins to unravel.

Struggling with his own demons, Leo's reluctant to take the case. Where do they even start with the vague testimony of a grief-stricken woman?

Allissa disagrees. She knows a woman on the edge when she sees one and takes the case alone. But, when things turn out to be more dangerous and volatile than she could have imagined, maybe she should have stayed well away.

Now writing on his home turf, London promises to be Luke Richardson's most intriguing novel so far. Pre-order

now to make sure you get your copy as soon as it's available.

GET LONDON NOW

WHAT HAPPENED IN KOH TAO?

READ THE SERIES PREQUEL NOVELLA FOR
FREE NOW

★★★★★

"Intense, thrilling, mysterious and captivating."

★★★★★

"The story grabs you, you're on the boat with your stomach pitching. As the story gathers pace the tension is palpable.

★★★★★ "

The evocative writing takes you to a place of white sand, the turquoise sea and tranquilly. But on an island of injustice and exploitation, tranquillity is the last thing Leo finds."

★★★★★

"Love and adventure collide in Thailand, love it!"

KOH TAO

Leo's looking for the perfect place to propose to the love of his life. When they arrive in the Thai tropical paradise of Koh Tao, he thinks he's found it.

But before he gets an answer, she's nowhere to be seen.

On searching the resort, his tranquillity turns to turmoil. Is it a practical joke? Has she run away? Or is it something much more sinister?

Set two years before Luke Richardson's international thriller series, this compulsive novella turns back the clock on an anxiety ridden man battling powerful forces in a foreign land.

KOH TAO is the prequel novella to Luke Richardson's international thriller series. Grab your copy for free and find out where it all began!

READ THE SERIES PREQUEL NOVELLA FOR FREE NOW

JOIN MY MAILING LIST

During the years it took me to write plan and my first book, I always looked to its publication as being the end of the process. The book would be out, and the story would be finished.

Since releasing Kathmandu in May 2019, I realised that putting the book into the world was actually just the start. Now I go on a new adventure with every conversation about my books.

Most of these conversations happen with people on my mailing list, and I'd love you to join too.

I send an email a couple of times a month in which I talk about my new releases, my inspirations and my travels.

I'll never spam you, or give your email address to anyone else, and of course you can leave at any time (although I hope you don't!)

Sign up now:

www.lukerichardsonauthor.com/mailinglist

THANK YOU

Thank you for reading *Istanbul*. Sharing my writing with you has been a dream of many years. Thank you for making it a reality.

As may come across in my writing, travelling, exploring and seeing the world is so important to me, as is coming home to my family and friends.

Although the words here are my own, the characters, experiences and some of the events described are wholly inspired by the people I've travelled beside. If we shared noodles from a street-food vendor, visited a temple together, played cards on a creaking overnight train, or had a beer in a back-street restaurant, you are forever in this book.

It is the intention of my writing to show that although the world is big and the unknown can be unsettling, there is so much good in it. Although some of the people in my stories are bad and evil — the story wouldn't be very interesting if they weren't — they're vastly outnumbered by the honesty, purity and kindness of the other characters. You don't have to look far to see this in the real world. I know that whenever I travel, it's the kindness of the people that I remember almost more than the place itself. Whether you're an experienced traveller, or you prefer your home turf, it's my hope that this story has taken you somewhere new and exciting.

Again, thank you for coming on the adventure with me, I hope to see you again.

Luke

P.S. A little warning, next time someone talks to you in the airport, be careful what you say, as you may end up in their book.

BOOK REVIEWS

If you've enjoyed this book I would appreciate a review.

Reviews are essential for three reasons. Firstly, they encourage people to take a chance on an author they've never heard of. Secondly, bookselling websites use them to decide what books to recommend through their search engine. And third, I love to hear what you think!

Having good reviews really can make a difference to new authors like me.

It'll take you no longer than two minutes, and will mean the world to me.

www.lukerichardsonauthor.com/reviews

Thank you.

Printed in Great Britain
by Amazon